The King of All That Is MAGIC

This book is a work of fiction. Names, characters, places, and incidents are the product of the author's imagination or are used fictitiously. Any resemblance to actual events, locales, corporate or government entities, facilities, or persons, living or dead, is coincidental.

The King of All That Is Magic
1st Edition

The King of All That Is MAGIC

ALEXANDER SAUNDERS

SHELBY, NC, USA

OTHER BOOKS BY
ALEXANDER SAUNDERS

Treasure of the Ancient Wizards

The Other Workers of Santa Claus

Table of Contents

ᴼPROLOGUE

Throughout time—across the history of humankind and every other lifeform in the universe—everyone has carried a secret. Sometimes for a good reason, sometimes for a bad one. Sometimes to protect others, and sometimes to know something they were never meant to.

There are also the great secrets and mysteries of life and the universe—truths humanity has yet to uncover, and perhaps never will. For not everything is meant to be explained. It doesn't help that humankind fears the unknown, even though that very fear has driven some of the darkest moments in history.

Whatever the reason, a secret is simply what it is.

But this isn't just a story about secrets. It's a story about two very different people—and the dangers and adventures they face together on a journey they never expected.

Then again, no one could have predicted what you're about to witness, either.

Jason Wolf was tall and a little chunky for a seventeen-year-old. His hair was short and dark, as were his eyes—a deep brown that seemed to hold both mischief and mystery. He usually dressed in dark clothes, and his voice carried an unusual mix of depth and lightness.

He came from a hardworking, hard-to-understand family—the kind that could make you laugh one minute and drive you crazy the next.

Natalia Summers, the same age as Jason, was one of those spoiled, self-centered girls who always got what she wanted. Her parents both had high-profile jobs that made them look—and live—as though they were better than everyone else.

Natalia had long, bright hair, flawless skin, and clear eyes. She wore only the latest fashions, and her voice was a mix of sweetness and steel.

But the most important thing to know about Jason and Natalia was that they had hated each other since kindergarten.

No one knew why—or how it started—or even who threw the first metaphorical punch. But everyone in the small coastal town of Northburg, Massachusetts, had grown used to it. Nothing could be done about their rivalry. Then again, no one really tried.

Northburg was their hometown, perched by the ocean, surrounded on the north and west by deep forests. It was a place full of shops, restaurants, and spots to hang out, have fun, and get into trouble.

The town had just one school—a combination of elementary, middle, and high school—and it was there that Jason and Natalia's paths collided daily.

Natalia was the most popular girl in Northburg. Nearly everyone in town adored her and would do anything for her... even if it meant breaking the rules.

With the help of her two best friends—Amanda and Samantha—who were more like sidekicks than actual friends, Natalia could do whatever she wanted. No one dared to say a word or even raise an eyebrow; most people simply turned a blind eye to the things she did.

Both girls were sixteen, different in their own ways, and had their fair share of unusual quirks.

Amanda had long, dyed red hair, small, sharp eyes, and lips always coated in bright red lipstick. She wore a lot of black and red clothing and avoided the sun whenever possible. Amanda also had an oddly strong craving for meat—especially rare—and a voice that carried the sharp tone of a typical "mean girl," though there was a hint of sweetness if you managed to get past her tough exterior.

Samantha, on the other hand, had dark skin, short hair, and a voice similar to Amanda's. She often suffered from strange, vivid nightmares and would wake to find her room looking as if a storm had torn through it. Even stranger, Samantha possessed wolf-like senses, and the pack of wolves that lived near her home seemed oddly drawn to her.

Neither Amanda nor Samantha understood the reasons behind their peculiar traits, but both knew they'd had them for as long as they could remember.

Still, with these two by her side, Natalia ruled—not just the school, but the entire town. And she treated everyone around her like dirt beneath her shoes.

Now, let's turn our attention back to the boy—Jason.

Jason was the kind of guy who had no friends, something Natalia and her friends had made sure of over the years. But he didn't mind. He preferred solitude, believing that if you were alone, no one could hurt you. For reasons no one quite understood, Jason was always disappearing. Whenever someone asked where he'd been, his only reply was a quiet, "None of your business."

This made a lot of people angry at him—but Jason didn't care.

When someone once tried to force an answer out of him, he shot back, "If you're always going to let Natalia Summers and her friends harass and humiliate me, why should I tell you where I disappear to?"

Then he stomped off, leaving everyone he despised fuming behind him. Jason didn't care—and he hadn't for years. He knew he could follow every rule and try to prove people wrong, but these days no one likes being proven wrong. Most people only see what they want to see.

Yes, he would get in trouble; but if that's what people expected from him, knowing he couldn't change their minds, it was just easier just to give them what they wanted. Still, when people finally get what they think they want, they don't always like the trouble that comes with it.

Whenever Jason and Natalia clashed, he was always the one who took the fall. Everyone believed her over him—even his own parents.

And that, he understand all too well. It's why he never had any respect for people who refused to hear his side of the story. No matter what he said, or even when proof showed it wasn't his fault, teachers, adults—all of them—just wanted someone to blame.

Now, Jason didn't have to worry much about his parents anymore. He hadn't lived with them for years, which had become something of a mystery in town. No one knew where he lived.

CHAPTER 1

NATALIA FINDS OUT

Now, our story begins on a clear spring afternoon. Natalia and her friends were walking home from cheerleading practice when they spotted one of the town's fast-food restaurants ahead.

"Hungry, girls?" Natalia asked.

"Starving!" Amanda and Samantha said together.

"Well, let's get something to eat."

The three of them stepped inside and joined the line.

When they reached the counter, the girl working there forced a polite smile and said, "What can I get for you?"

She spoke with extra politeness—mostly because she hated those three.

"Oh, you know what we want, Sasha," Natalia said rudely.

"Or has the smell of fast food made you forget?" Amanda added.

Sasha ignored them and kept working.

After giving their order, the girls found a table by the window.

As they began to eat, Natalia took a second bite of her burger and sneered, "Can you believe her?"

"Well," Samantha said after sipping her soda, "she's still the new girl, and she likes hanging around someone like Jason."

"Makes them both a couple of losers," Amanda said, nibbling a few fries. "Losers no one wants to be around."

All three laughed in a way that sounded deliberately cruel.

After a few seconds, Natalia continued, "I've noticed he's been trying to ask a lot of girls out these past few months."

"But why?" the other two chorused.

"I don't know," Natalia said, taking a sip of her drink. "But a lot of people in this town are still wondering where he lives and where he disappears to."

"Do you?" they asked in unison.

"Of course not!" Natalia scoffed, spitting out a chunk of her burger. "But it would be hilarious to find out his secrets and spread them all over town."

"Haven't you done enough damage to him already, Natalia? Or do you just enjoy what you do?"

It was Sasha—the girl behind the counter—who had spoken. She'd heard every word. At her voice, everyone turned.

Natalia stood from her seat and called across the restaurant, "What's this I hear from you, Sasha? You actually care about another loser? I thought you had more sense than that."

Normally, someone working in a place like this would never dare to talk back. But this time, Sasha knew she was doing the right thing. And sometimes, doing the right thing matters more than whatever comes next.

"No," Sasha said firmly. "I'm just saying that because of you, he has no one to talk to—and not even his own parents—"

"It sounds like you do care," Natalia interrupted in a mocking tone, shooting Sasha a dark look.

Sasha met it without flinching.

Just as Sasha opened her mouth to respond, a door swung open behind her and a bald man stepped out.

"Sasha, in my office. Now."

She obeyed without hesitation—but not before giving Natalia one last glare, which Natalia returned with equal venom.

When Sasha was gone, Natalia smirked and sat back down.

"Now, girls, where were we?"

"We were talking about how funny it would be if everyone in town knew where Jason lived," Samantha said.

That made Natalia's smile turn wicked.

After finishing the last bite of her burger, she said, "Oh, yes. But how do we do that? Hardly anyone ever sees him around town, and he's only at school a few times a week. Any ideas?"

"Well," Amanda said, lowering her voice, "someone told me they saw him a few days ago with two strange-looking people—wearing weird clothes—and before they could get a good look... they all just disappeared."

That made Natalia pause for a few seconds before saying, "Yes, that's something everyone keeps saying—like last Friday, when he walked out of homeroom without an explanation. Mrs. F told him to sit down, but he ignored her. She followed him down the hallway, and when she came back, he was gone. She actually said, 'How did he vanish like that?' And by Monday morning, we all expected him to be in serious trouble. But the way Mrs. F acted— it was like it never even happened."

"I even asked her about it that same day," Amanda said, "when I gave her my homework and asked for a night off."

Natalia frowned slightly as she finished, "When I asked her about it, she just said she didn't know what I was talking about."

When both girls asked why, Natalia replied, "Well, why is it that every time he disappears, runs off, or skips school, people notice—but when it comes time to punish him, everyone suddenly forgets?"

Their conversation ended there, and they decided to leave.

Later that day, they were in Natalia's bedroom—a room larger than most seventeen-year-old girls could dream of, a clear sign that her parents were well off.

As the three girls sat on her oversized bed, Amanda asked, "Are you sure your parents are okay with us staying another night?"

"How many times do I have to say it?" Natalia replied, her laugh sharp and hollow. "My parents are working late again tonight. They're never home—and even if they were, they always let me do whatever I want."

As she said this, a flicker of sadness crossed her face—one she quickly hid from her friends.

Even so, when people like Natalia chose a path like hers, it was usually because they were hurting inside—feeling alone, misunderstood, and unwilling to admit it to themselves or anyone else. That pain often became the reason they inflicted it on others. Even though Natalia was a spoiled brat who treated everyone around her as if they were beneath her, deep down she hated the person she had become. But after living that way for so long, she believed there was no turning back.

Of course, that wasn't true. It's never too late to change who you are or turn over a new leaf. There's always hope for everyone, even if it's hard to find. That's the problem with people these days—so few are willing to try.

However, when Samantha repeated Amanda's question, Natalia grew annoyed.

"Guys, I told you already," she said.

"It's not that," Samantha replied before Amanda could speak. "It's just that every time we sleep over—"

"Don't worry about it," Natalia interrupted.

She knew exactly what they were hinting at and quickly changed the subject, saying she wanted to update some of her things and that this was the perfect chance to do it.

A few minutes later, the three girls drifted back to the topic of Jason Wolf.

As they talked, a wicked smile spread across Natalia's face.

"I don't know what we'll find when we figure out where he disappears to," she said, "but I bet it'll be something that ruins his life—forever."

"So," Amanda asked, "should we make sure our phones are fully charged? You know... so we can take a few pictures?"

Both Amanda and Samantha climbed into their sleeping bags at the end of Natalia's bed.

As Natalia turned off the light, she grinned in the dark and said softly, "Oh, yes."

They all quickly fell asleep. That night, Natalia had a dream—a strange, fragmented dream that made no sense to her. Flashes of images appeared all at once, chaotic and vivid, until she woke with a start. She tried to remember what she'd seen, but within seconds, it was gone. So she sighed, rolled over, and drifted back to sleep.

The next day at Northburg School, during lunch, Natalia and her friends were on the lookout for Jason—something that wasn't easy most days.

The cafeteria, like most school cafeterias, was a miserable place to be. It felt like eating inside a giant, windowless box that reeked of rotten eggs and month-old garbage. The air hung thick and sour. Located at the very center of the school, the cafeteria had no windows—just a few small skylights that barely let in enough light to keep the room from feeling like a dungeon. It was easily the gloomiest, most unpleasant spot in the entire building. As for the food, it was the kind of thing that made most parents pack lunches for their kids. Like many public schools, the meals here were cheap, barely edible, and often left students with stomach aches—or worse. Honestly, if the government put half as much effort into funding schools, hospitals, and people who needed help, maybe kids wouldn't have to eat that kind of food in the first place.

Natalia, Amanda, and Samantha spent the first few minutes of lunch searching the room until they spotted Jason—sitting all the way at the back of the cafeteria with Sasha.

The two of them spoke in low whispers, careful that no one could overhear.

Sasha, with her long blonde hair and soft pink lips, always looked half-friendly, half-sad. Even her clothes reflected that—simple but graceful, a little bright, a little somber. Her voice carried that same tone—part stern, part strong, but always steady.

Nevertheless, the three girls managed to get close enough to overhear what Jason and Sasha were saying—without being seen.

"Sorry you got fired yesterday," Jason said quietly.

Sasha giggled.

"I was going to quit anyway. I really hated that job. Honestly, I hate any job in this realm. The working conditions are awful. I just feel like I failed you, and—"

Jason stopped her before she could finish.

"You didn't. You've never failed me. I'd trust you with anything. I'm grateful you're my advisor."

They both laughed softly.

Then Jason's tone grew somber.

"I just have to accept that it's going to happen; but I'm not going to end it by letting him take over."

"And it won't," Sasha replied firmly.

The three girls didn't understand what any of this meant, but they did find it amusing that Sasha had been fired for talking back.

However, their laughter died down when they heard Sasha say, "Still, after lunch, I need to get you out of here and ready for the celebration."

Jason looked uneasy.

"I still don't understand why they can't have one celebration or event without—"

"Sire," Sasha interrupted, cutting him off. "You know as well as everyone else that the celebration can't start without you. It wouldn't be any fun!

Besides, are you forgetting the main reason this is happening? The reason you wanted it in the first place?"

Jason wanted to find a way out of this but finally sighed and said, "You're right. I just wish there were another way… but I guess there isn't."

Unbeknownst to them, Natalia and her friends were completely shocked by what they'd just overheard.

Samantha leaned in close and whispered, just loud enough for Amanda and Natalia to hear, "When they say 'celebration,' do you think they mean a party?"

"And why did she call him *sire*?" Amanda added, her eyes wide.

Natalia stayed silent, trying to piece it all together.

After a moment, she muttered, "A celebration always means a party—but who in their right mind would invite *those two* to one?"

"Do you think," Amanda began slowly, "this has something to do with where he disappears to?"

Natalia smiled, the corners of her mouth curling mischievously.

"I think it does. Which means we'll be leaving school after lunch, too. And soon, everyone will finally know where he goes."

"Are you sure we can do that?" Samantha asked, frowning.

Natalia looked at her as if the question were ridiculous.

"We're cheerleaders, Samantha. Everyone knows that if you're one of the few who brings glory to your school—or your town—you can get away with anything. Why do you think none of the teachers ever take Jason's side when we give him a hard time?"

And that, sadly, is a fact—not just here, but in schools everywhere. Too many teachers turn a blind eye to bullying. Even after school, when Jason still lived with his parents, he couldn't walk around town without some creep trying to harass or mock him. He couldn't forgive the people he went to school with—or the staff who let it happen. Not once did they stop anyone from bullying him, even when they saw it happening. When Jason finally fought back, they punished him instead—lying to his parents about what was really going on.

Natalia and her friends listened as Jason said to Sasha, "Sorry, this is the fifth celebration this month, and I'm getting a bit tired of them."

"I know," Sasha replied gently, her voice soft and understanding. "Everyone knows that, but you have to be there."

"I know," he said, cutting her off before she could finish. "But I'm not doing much this time."

"You don't have to, *Sire,*" Sasha said with a small smile.

"All the same," he said with a yawn, "I hope that once this plan works, I can finally rest for a few days."

"Why are you saying that?" she teased, giggling.

"Because it's been nonstop for weeks," he said. "I think I deserve a break after everything I've done."

"You do," Sasha agreed warmly. "But right now, Sire, let's get you out of here and get you ready for the celebration."

After finishing their food, they stood up, tossed their trash, and left the cafeteria.

Natalia and her friends followed quietly, keeping to the shadows. They trailed the two down a long, dim hallway—the kind of place few students ever went.

Sasha and Jason glanced around, making sure no one was nearby. Believing the coast was clear, they relaxed.

But from the shadows, the three girls watched in stunned silence as Sasha began to speak in a strange, rhythmic language they couldn't understand.

Then, before their eyes, a massive swirl of color burst into existence—like a glowing hole in midair.

A portal? They wondered.

Just as Sasha and Jason stepped through it, the three girls hurried forward.

"What is going on? What did they just do?" Natalia demanded, staring into the swirling light.

Amanda and Samantha looked just as shocked as she was.

Before they could make sense of it, Amanda said, "We might as well go through and see what's on the other side."

"Why would we do that?" Natalia snapped.

Before she could calm herself, Samantha shouted, "We'd better decide now—this thing's about to close!"

Without another thought, the three girls leapt into the portal just as it began to seal shut.

What they saw next nearly made them faint. They found themselves in the middle of a vast forest—unlike any forest they had ever seen. The trees looked younger, stronger, almost alive. Once or twice, one of the girls could have sworn she saw them shift positions—or even bend toward one another, whispering in low, creaking voices.

Each of them was thinking the same thing. *Where are we?*

Before any of them could speak, a deep voice grunted, "If you three are here for the celebration, follow the Changing Path and you'll arrive in no time."

"Who said that?" Natalia gasped.

They spun around, searching for the source of the voice.

"Look behind you," it said again.

Slowly, they turned—and froze.

At first, they thought it was their imagination or someone playing a prank. But then, one of the towering trees stepped forward, roots shifting like feet.

The girls screamed and stumbled back, eyes wide in disbelief.

The tree didn't seem to notice—or care. It spoke again, its bark-like mouth moving as it said, "The celebration is straight ahead, in the great clearing. I'm sure His Majesty—the King of All That Is Magic—will be honored to have you there."

"The King?" Natalia whispered, her voice trembling.

The tree turned to leave and rejoin the others, but not before saying, "Just follow the path to the celebration—but you might want to hurry, before the real fun begins."

After it pointed them in the right direction, the girls started walking.

As they went, Natalia glanced down and said, "I can see why they call this the Changing Path."

"Why is that?" her two friends asked in unison.

Natalia pointed downward, and when Samantha and Amanda looked, they saw that the ground beneath them was shifting in color and texture—changing every few seconds as if alive.

Despite their unease, they couldn't help but think it was fascinating. The path continued to transform beneath their feet as they walked, glowing and rippling like liquid light. After a while, a hint of worry crept into their excitement.

"I just hope Jason and Sasha can tell us what this place is," Amanda said softly, "and what's really going on."

Natalia laughed.

"Do you really think *they* know where we are?"

"They're the ones who opened that hole and brought us here," Samantha said, glancing at the strange, shifting trees surrounding them.

Before Natalia could reply, the sound of laughter and voices carried through the forest—people cheering, talking, celebrating.

"A great day for it," someone said.

"You can say that again," another replied.

"Hope it goes on all day."

"Let's hope he'll allow it."

"He might."

"Here, here!"

The three girls froze, exchanging glances. The voices were close now—too close.

"I guess we're almost there," Natalia said, her voice a mixture of excitement and disbelief.

Just as they were about to move forward, Amanda stopped and said, "Do you really think we should keep going this way?"

Her friends looked at her in confusion.

"I just mean," she continued, "if Jason and Sasha see us, they're not going to let us come anywhere near... whatever this thing is."

She trailed off, unsure how to explain the uneasy feeling twisting in her stomach. Natalia felt it too.

"You're right," Natalia finally said.

So instead of following the path to the very end, the girls slipped off the trail and crept through a cluster of trees that seemed to be softly snoring in their sleep. As they got closer to the sounds of celebration, they pulled out their phones, ready to record what they might find.

They soon reached a large, shadowed clearing where they could hide without being seen. It was a good thing, too—because what they saw next made them drop their phones. By some miracle, neither phone cracked nor broke. The sight before them was something no one—least of all three ordinary girls like them—would have believed unless they saw it with their own eyes. Before them was a gathering of magical creatures. Witches, wizards, goblins, dwarfs, werewolves, vampires, merfolk, forest nymphs, hags, satyrs, trolls, ogres, giants— every being ever mentioned in fairy tales or fantasy books was right there before them, alive and real.

The girls stood frozen in disbelief. This was impossible.

As a few centaurs trotted into the clearing, followed by ghouls, fauns, and other strange beings, Amanda whispered, "This has got to be a dream or something. It can't be real. These creatures don't exist."

But they did exist. And no matter how hard the girls tried to convince themselves otherwise—or even pinch their arms in hopes of waking up—it was no use.

Just as they began to accept the truth, Sasha appeared out of nowhere, stepping onto a raised platform they hadn't noticed before.

At first, they barely recognized her. She was dressed in flowing black robes and a tall, pointed hat—clearly witch's attire.

"She's a witch?" Amanda whispered in shock.

"Well, that explains a lot," Samantha muttered.

Before they could say anything else, Sasha raised her hand for silence and spoke in a commanding voice.

"Magical citizens of the Magical Realm, His Royal Highness—the King of All That Is Magic, Jason Wolf—will now speak."

The girls gasped as Jason stepped forward, greeted by thunderous applause from the crowd of creatures. He wore deep red robes embroidered with gold stripes, and a golden crown set with a bright ruby rested on his head.

He looked radiant—confident—as he smiled and waved to the magical beings before him.

CHAPTER 2
PROBLEMS FOR THE KING

"King!" Natalia gasped. "He's a *king*?" The shock nearly made all three girls faint. Of all the things they'd expected, this was the very last.

When the crowd finally grew quiet, Jason stepped forward and said, his voice ringing through the clearing, "My friends, I have only one thing to say—let the celebration begin!"

The moment the words left his mouth, a magnificent throne shimmered into existence, and Jason took his seat, watching as his people began to celebrate with wild joy.

Music filled the air. Creatures of every kind—trolls, elves, fairies, and goblins—danced and sang. Laughter echoed through the clearing.

A few seconds into the celebration, several ogres, gremlins, and elves noticed their king sitting quietly, smiling faintly as he observed them.

A young female ogre stepped forward and asked in a surprisingly sweet, piglike voice, "Your Highness, aren't you going to join us?"

"Not today," Jason said with a weary smile, leaning back on his throne.

"But why?" the ogre asked again, tilting her head.

Before Jason could respond, Sasha stepped in smoothly and said on his behalf, "His Royal Highness is a bit worn out today, due to certain matters in the Human Realm."

The ogre nodded knowingly.

"That girl who gives him trouble—is she at it again?"

Sasha sighed and nodded.

"Not just that. He's exhausted. He's done so much for us already."

"I'm just tired right now," Jason said, "but that doesn't mean you should all stop having fun. So please, everyone—stop worrying about me and enjoy yourselves! Eat, drink, dance, and have fun!"

And so they did.

As the celebration carried on, Natalia whispered to her friends, "I still can't believe this."

"Well, what are we going to do?" Samantha asked nervously.

"What do you mean?" Natalia and Amanda said together.

Samantha swallowed hard.

"If Jason sees us, he'll probably have us humiliated—or worse!"

"What makes you say that?" Natalia asked, frowning.

Amanda jumped in before Samantha could answer.

"Have you forgotten how much grief we've given him over the years? If he's really respected and honored here, they might do something terrible to us!"

Natalia fell silent, thinking about that. The realization unsettled her more than she wanted to admit.

Meanwhile, Jason sat slouched in his throne, his eyes half-closed.

He was on the edge of sleep when Sasha leaned close and said softly, "Forgive me for waking you, Your Majesty, but—"

"I know the reason, Siberanna," he interrupted, calling her by her true name. He yawned deeply and added, "But everything looks fine for now."

"That may be true, Sire," she said seriously, "but you can never be too careful, and since—"

She didn't finish.

Jason suddenly stiffened, his eyes snapping open as he noticed several werewolves nearby sniffing the air.

He turned sharply toward them, pointing in their direction.

His voice rose, loud and tense.

"What's going on? What's happening?"

"We don't know, Sire!" one of the werewolves said, continuing to sniff the air along with several others. "But we smell something."

At his words, the entire clearing fell silent. Another werewolf stepped forward and said, "It's something… half strange, half normal."

"Something that rarely comes to the Magical Realm," added a female werewolf, her ears twitching as she sniffed again.

Jason exchanged a tense glance with Siberanna before saying, "It can't be *him*—he always makes an entrance. Find out what it is, immediately."

"At once, Sire," several of them replied before fanning out and sniffing the air.

The crowd murmured nervously as the werewolves prowled closer and closer to the tree line. Natalia, Amanda, and Samantha exchanged terrified looks, trying not to breathe too loudly.

Then one of the werewolves stopped suddenly and growled, "The scent is coming from *that* direction."

He pointed straight toward the spot where the girls were hiding.

Before they could react—before they could even think about running—three wizards and a witch raised their wands and fired a powerful spell. A burst of blinding light exploded through the shadows, striking the girls' hiding place. In an instant, the three girls were thrown forward, tumbling face-first onto the ground.

Gasps and whispers rippled through the crowd as everyone caught sight of the intruders. Jason froze, his expression darkening with anger. When he finally spoke, his voice was sharp and commanding.

"Seize them—and bring them to me at once."

At his command, two hobgoblins, a wizard, and a troll rushed forward. Each grabbed one of the girls by the back of her shirt.

"Get up," one of them snarled. "Now."

As the girls were dragged through the crowd, the magical creatures surrounding them began to mutter among themselves.

"You think they're just humans who wandered into our world by accident?"

"They might be a few of Campbell's followers."

"Can't be—he only has two minions."

"And there's no trace of dark magic on them."

"But there *is* a smell of human wickedness about them."

While the creatures whispered, Jason turned to Siberanna, his eyes narrowing as he watched the three girls he despised being pulled toward him.

"What in the name of magic are *they* doing here?" he demanded. "I thought you said we weren't being followed!"

He waited for an answer, his tone edged with anger and disbelief. Siberanna looked just as shocked as he was.

"I don't know, Sire," she admitted. "I must have been so focused on getting you here safely that I didn't sense we were being followed."

Before Jason could respond, the four magical beings dragged the girls forward and threw them to the ground at his feet.

"As you ordered, Your Majesty," one of them said with a bow. "The three intruders."

"And from the look on your face, Your Majesty," one of the hobgoblins began cautiously, "I think you—"

Jason raised a finger for silence. He wasn't in the mood to explain himself.

Before anyone else could speak, he leaned back on his throne and said coolly, "Well, well, well… look what the dragon puked up."

The three girls didn't understand what he meant, though they'd heard him say things like that before. One of them started to speak—but before she could, several witches and wizards appeared behind them, wands raised.

"You will bow when you speak to His Majesty," one of the witches commanded.

This was the last thing any of them wanted to do—but under the wizards' watchful eyes, they did it, kneeling reluctantly while keeping their gaze locked on Jason.

Jason watched with clear satisfaction, though his expression hardened as he spoke again.

"I'd like to say it's good to see you three," he said, his tone dripping with venom, "but that would be a lie—and I don't like lying. So tell me… how did you get into this realm?"

His voice was cold and heavy with anger—so much so that even some of the magical creatures nearby flinched.

The girls were stunned. They had never heard him speak this way before.

Natalia, however, couldn't stop herself.

In her usual defiant tone, she snapped, "Hey—you can't talk to us like that!"

Gasps echoed through the crowd. No one in the Magical Realm would ever dare speak to the king that way. Then, as murmurs spread among the onlookers, realization began to dawn on them. These must be the three girls who had tormented their king in the Human Realm.

Just as Jason was about to speak, Siberanna stepped forward, raising her wand and pointing it at the three girls.

"He can speak to you however he likes," she said sharply. "You're on his turf now, *Natalia*, and if you—"

"Are you threatening me, Sasha?" Natalia interrupted, glaring at her.

Instead of backing down, both Siberanna and Jason laughed.

"Sasha's not my real name," Siberanna said, her voice firm. "It's *Siberanna*. And not only am I one of the most powerful witches in this realm, but I am also the royal advisor to His Majesty, King Jason Wolf—ruler of the entire Magical Realm."

At her words, Natalia looked at Amanda and Samantha, both wearing the same wide-eyed expression of disbelief.

"You can't be serious," Natalia said. "*Him?* A king? Why—"

"If you finish that sentence," Siberanna interrupted, her tone dripping with menace, "I'll turn you and your friends into jelly and save you for a peanut butter and jelly sandwich."

The crowd chuckled nervously, though the threat sounded far too real.

Before anyone else could speak, Jason noticed an old wizard in the crowd laughing.

He frowned and said, "Moongum, may I ask what's so funny?"

The wizard stepped forward, pushing through the crowd until he stood before the king, Siberanna, and the three human girls.

He was of average height, with a neatly trimmed white beard and a kind but mischievous face. His silver robes shimmered faintly under the magical lights, and his tall, matching hat tilted slightly to one side.

Speaking in a calm, businesslike tone, he said, "Well, Your Majesty, I don't know if this is true, but I'll say it anyway. You've often mentioned that this human girl has been nothing but trouble for you since your kindergarten days in the Human Realm, correct?"

"Yes," Jason said curtly, his eyes narrowing.

Both he and Natalia exchanged wary glances, wondering where this was going.

"Well, Sire," Moongum continued, stroking his beard, "according to the *Chronicles of Ancient Magic*—the record of all knowledge across time and

24

the realms—when two humans have hated each other for so long, it usually means they are, in truth, deeply in love."

The words hung in the air. It was the *last* thing Jason ever wanted to hear.

Even Natalia's face turned bright red. "*Me?* In love with Jason Wolf? That's—"

"As a matter of fact," Moongum interrupted cheerfully, "you're already showing the same signs described in the chronicles—the same signs human girls show when trying to hide their feelings."

Natalia was speechless.

Jason, however, ignored her reaction and snapped, "Moongum, in case you—or anyone else here—has forgotten, I *hate* these three. Especially Natalia. And I'd like to know why you're bringing this up now, of all times—*and* in front of her!"

"Because, Sire," Moongum said, his voice suddenly grave, "time is short for you. If you don't act soon, it will be too late. And you know what's at stake if what we all fear comes to pass."

A heavy silence fell over the clearing.

Finally, Jason said in a low, uneasy tone, "I understand that, but—"

"What are you talking about?" Natalia demanded.

"It's none of your business, Natalia," he snapped.

His words hit her like a slap. She opened her mouth to argue, but before she could, something strange began to happen.

A ripple of unease spread through the crowd as heads turned upward. Jason's expression darkened.

Oh no... not now, he thought grimly.

A dark cloud began to swirl above them, growing larger and blacker by the second. As it spread across the sky, Jason rose from his throne, his calm demeanor slipping into panic. Lightning cracked across the clearing, and the celebration erupted into chaos. Screams echoed as magical creatures scattered in fear.

"Warriors!" Jason shouted. "Prepare yourselves for battle!"

At his command, dozens of witches and wizards drew their wands. Ogres, trolls, and giants armed themselves with clubs, swords, daggers, shields, bows, and arrows. The dark cloud thickened, swallowing the sunlight until day turned to night.

"What's happening?" Natalia cried. "What's going on?"

Before anyone could answer, three bolts of lightning struck the ground with deafening force. Creatures jumped aside as the smoke cleared—revealing two wizards and a witch standing at the center of the scorched earth, wicked smiles curling across their faces. Even Natalia and her friends, inexperienced as they were, could tell at once—these newcomers were not good people. They were the very definition of evil.

The one standing in the middle had skin that looked scorched—burned and blistered as though he'd spent years standing in flames. His face was rough and dark, his head completely bald, and a thin, scraggly beard clung to his chin. His hands were filthy, his nails black with soot, and he wore dark purple robes with black boots caked in ash. When he spoke, his voice was a grotesque mix between a frog's croak and a pig's snort.

At the sight of him, Jason rose from his throne and stepped forward.

"Campbell," he said sharply, "what are you, Gorman, and Jeffgon doing here?"

Campbell laughed, a harsh, grating sound.

"What's this? You're not happy to see us, Jason?"

"Do you really want me to answer that?" Jason replied coldly.

At that, Gorman let out a shrill laugh and said, "Well, someone's in a bad mood today!"

Her remark sent the other two wizards into fits of laughter, as if expecting the crowd to join them. But instead, their mockery only stirred anger among the gathered magical creatures—some even hissed or spat in disgust that the three had dared to show their faces here.

Gorman was a ghastly old woman with a cruel, twisted face and piercing, hate-filled eyes. Her wrinkled hands were as dirty as her personality, and she wiped them absently on her black-and-green striped robes. A tattered, mismatched witch's hat sat crookedly atop her greasy gray hair. Her voice was a grating blend of cackle and scream.

Jeffgon, by contrast, looked younger than the other two, though no cleaner. His face and hands were smeared with grime, and his robes and boots looked as though they hadn't been washed in years. When he spoke, his tone was that of a nasty, insolent teenager.

As the three dark figures laughed together, Jason ignored them and turned to head back to his throne—only to notice Natalia had sat in it.

"Get off my throne," he growled.

She jumped to her feet immediately.

Jason dropped into the seat with a heavy sigh and muttered loud enough for everyone to hear, "Well, well... things just can't get any worse, can they?"

"Why's that?" Campbell asked mockingly, his voice dripping with sarcasm.

Jason shot him a glare.

"First, three humans I *despise* somehow find their way into my realm—something I thought impossible."

His eyes flicked toward Natalia, Amanda, and Samantha as he continued, "And now, you three show up."

Before anyone could respond, Siberanna stepped forward, wand raised, and pointed it directly at Campbell, Gorman, and Jeffgon.

"The three of you were *forbidden*—by order of Queen Allison Norton herself—to attend any magical celebrations!" she declared.

Jeffgon smirked, his yellowed teeth glinting.

"Do you really think we have nothing better to do than obey some *so-called human* who everyone wants ruling this realm?"

"You know why it had to be that way," Siberanna said sternly.

Just as she was about to continue, Jason rose from his throne and stepped in front of her.

The crowd fell silent as he said, "Tell me something. Do you three *enjoy* making me angry and testing my patience? Because I've had enough trouble from you in my time as king—and now I have this to say."

"Which is?" Campbell said with mock surprise.

Jason smiled coldly.

Then, at the top of his voice, he shouted, "Get them!"

Chaos erupted. Spells flew in every direction as witches, wizards, trolls, and ogres charged the intruders. Campbell and his minions scrambled for their wands, barely fending off the assault.

As he deflected a barrage of magic, Campbell shouted toward the throne, "What is the meaning of this?"

"What do you think, Campbell?" Jason called back, joining the fight. "I'm doing what I've been trying to do for *years*."

"You mean... this is a trap?" Gorman shrieked, blasting away two elves and a goblin trying to restrain her.

Jason nodded, confident and focused.

The girls from the Human Realm were even laughing at the sight.

"Wow, Campbell," Jason said with a smirk. "Your minions actually got it right this time. Yes—

this *was* a trap. The whole celebration was just a way to lure you here."

"A perfect plan, Your Majesty," Siberanna added with a proud grin.

She stayed close, ensuring Jason didn't rush into the fight himself.

"You think you're funny, Jason?" Campbell spat as he battled two trolls and a banshee at once.

Jason's voice cracked with emotion.

"I *know* I'm funny, Campbell, because this time, you won't escape. This time, you'll answer for your crimes!"

"We'll see about that," Campbell growled.

He and his followers shoved their attackers back and raised their wands skyward, chanting a dark spell.

Jason knew the spell instantly—he'd seen it too many times before.

He hurled orbs of light toward them and shouted, "You're not getting away this time!"

But his magic was reflected back. Campbell and his minions began to fade, their forms flickering in and out. They hurled a blinding beam of light toward the throne. Jason managed to block it, but it bought them the time they needed. And then—they were gone.

Jason lunged forward, ready to pursue, but Siberanna and Natalia held him back.

"Let me go! Let me go!" he shouted.

"They're not worth it, Jason," Natalia said softly. "Just forget it."

"She's right, Sire," Siberanna added.

Jason stopped, breathing heavily, watching the horizon where the dark trio had vanished. Then, overcome by frustration, he let out a roar of anger so powerful it echoed through the entire realm.

When at last he calmed, both Siberanna and Natalia guided him back to his throne.

Siberanna placed a steadying hand on his shoulder and said, "We'll get them next time, Sire."

"If there *is* a next time," Jason muttered bitterly.

For a long moment he sat there, quiet and brooding.

When he finally rose, he faced the gathered crowd and said, "Everyone, I'm afraid the plan didn't go as I hoped. Campbell escaped... so the celebration is now over."

"Are you serious, Sire?" many disappointed voices asked.

Before Jason could reply, Siberanna stepped forward.

"Most of you knew the real purpose of this celebration—"

"And since it didn't succeed," Jason added, "I'm ending it. Please begin cleaning up. I'm sorry, but..."

His voice trailed off. There was no need for further explanation. Seeing the sorrow on their king's face, everyone quietly began to clear the area. Jason wanted to help, but his people insisted they would handle it. So he sat back on his throne, lost in thought, wondering if he would ever truly succeed—and what might happen the next time he faced Campbell and his minions.

He was pulled from his thoughts by an unexpected sound: Amanda's laughter. She and Samantha were helping the others—Amanda working with a group of vampires, Samantha with several werewolves. Their cooperation surprised him. He'd never imagined those two would help anyone unless there was something in it for them. But what surprised him most was that Natalia remained by his side.

Siberanna was busy overseeing the cleanup, breaking up small fights between creatures arguing over leftover food and drink. When she saw everything was under control, she went to check on Moongum, who had taken a few bad hits during the fight.

Jason sat with his head resting in one hand, lost in thought.

After a while, Natalia said softly, "Are you alright?"

Her kindness startled him.

He turned to her and said, "I've been better. When did *you* start caring?"

She didn't take offense.

"Well... after seeing all of this—and everything you've gone through—"

He raised a hand to stop her, removed his crown, and scratched his head.

"Sorry. This thing itches sometimes."

"It does?" she said, surprised.

He smiled faintly.

"Just because something *looks* good doesn't mean it *feels* good. I often wonder if the kings and queens before me felt the same way—or even the rulers back in the Human Realm."

"Never thought about that," she said with a laugh. "But as I was saying... seeing you like this made me realize I really am a—"

"Self-centered, mean-spirited, lying—"

"I get it," she interrupted quickly. "You're right, Jason. I *am* all those things and more. That's why I mean it when I say I'm really sorry for everything I've said and done to you."

"Are you?" he asked quietly, still looking away.

"Yes," she said. "And I want to prove it."

"How?" he said in a cold voice, turning to face her.

"By helping you capture Campbell and his two minions."

Jason stared at her in disbelief.

"Jason... I mean, Your Majesty," she added, bowing her head slightly.

He blinked, surprised by her tone and respect.

"I'm just shocked," he said, "that you're suddenly being *nice* to me. Especially after everything you've done."

"Treated you like dirt, I know," she said quickly. "But after seeing what you deal with—"

"I get the picture," he interrupted. "And I kind of like this side of you. I just hope it's not an act."

"It's not," she said with a nervous laugh. "Seeing you in action today just... changed how I see you."

Both fell silent, watching the cleanup. Magic made the work easier, but much of the debris was enchanted, so the process was slow and careful.

When the work was finally done, Jason rose again, with Natalia at his side. Siberanna returned to stand beside him.

"My friends," Jason began, "our plan to capture Campbell, Gorman, and Jeffgon worked *almost* as intended—but they escaped. I'm sorry I failed you again."

"You didn't fail us, Sire," said a young gorgon with a gentle voice.

"We failed you," added a troll beside her, his tone solemn.

"No," Jason said firmly. "I'm your king. It's my duty to take responsibility for what happens in this realm."

"That's not fair," Natalia said softly, placing a hand on his shoulder.

Siberanna sighed.

"I can't believe I'm saying this, but as much as I'd like to agree with you, Natalia, His Majesty is right. A true ruler takes both the praise and the blame."

Natalia didn't like it, but she understood.

Siberanna turned back to Jason.

"Your Majesty, we nearly had them. This is the closest we've ever come."

Jason nodded slowly.

"Which means they'll stay hidden for a while— until they think our guard is down."

"We'll get them, Sire," Siberanna said. "It may take time, but we will."

"Maybe I can help," Natalia offered.

Siberanna frowned.

"What is she talking about, Sire?"

"She wants to help," Jason said dryly.

"If you're serious," Siberanna told Natalia, "you must understand—you'll have to spend a lot of time away from the Human Realm."

"I understand."

"And you'll miss school... and plenty of other things."

"I don't mind," Natalia said firmly.

Siberanna stared at her, unimpressed.

"I don't get you, Natalia."

"I know," Natalia said. "But I'm not asking for kindness or forgiveness. I know I've been awful to the king, but after everything I've seen, I want to make things right."

The crowd began to applaud. Even Jason managed a small smile.

"I hope you understand what you're getting into," he said.

"I do," she replied.

He explained the dangers of Campbell and his followers. Though it frightened her, she didn't back down.

"Well," she said at last, "it sounds like a challenge to me."

Jason sighed, but before he could argue, Siberanna stepped in.

"Sire, let her help."

Jason groaned and sat back down.

"This is no place for a human—especially one who's caused me more trouble than Campbell ever has."

"All the more reason I *should* help," Natalia shot back.

Jason gave a tired laugh.

"I'm not going to win this argument, am I?"

"You think?" the two girls said in unison.

Siberanna chuckled.

"Sire, you said it yourself—you'd take all the help you could get."

Jason sighed again.

"I did say that, didn't I?"

Siberanna smiled.

"What are your orders now, Your Majesty?"

Jason stood and said, "You may all go home."

As the crowd dispersed, Amanda and Samantha approached.

"Sire," Samantha said, "we need to tell you something."

Jason nodded.

"Go on."

Samantha took a deep breath.

"Some of your people said I have the signs of becoming a werewolf."

"And I have the signs of becoming a vampire," Amanda added.

Jason's eyes widened.

"What?"

Siberanna explained gently.

"Sometimes, in your realm, humans are born with traces of magic—a spark that can grow into something greater. When they reach a certain age, they can choose whether to embrace it or not."

"Not many do," she continued. "But those who do often live extraordinary lives here."

"Which is why," Samantha said, "we're not going back to the Human Realm."

"What?" Natalia gasped.

Jason answered quietly, "Once a human accepts their magical nature, their old life is erased forever."

Natalia's heart sank.

"That means if they stay... I'll have no friends."

Jason softened toward Natalia for the first time.

"You'll make new ones. You're the most popular girl in Northburg, remember?"

She smiled faintly but didn't reply.

"Would you like me to send you home?" Siberanna asked gently.

Natalia nodded. In an instant, the world vanished—and she was back in her bedroom.

"What just happened?" she gasped.

"Nothing special," Siberanna said with a small smile. "Just magical teleporting."

As she turned to leave, Natalia said, "Wait—please don't go."

Siberanna stopped.

"Why not?"

"I just want to talk," Natalia said quietly. "I want to know how hard I'll have to work to prove myself to the king. I want him to know how sorry I am."

Siberanna studied her for a long moment.

"It will take time," she said gently. "Especially after what happened today. But perhaps... he'll see the change in you."

"I hope so," Natalia whispered.

Siberanna nodded.

"For now, rest. The king has bigger problems."

"What do you mean?" Natalia asked, uneasy.

"Well," Siberanna said gravely, "you know how the king has been trying to find someone special?"

Natalia froze.

"He must marry before the end of this year," Siberanna continued. "If he doesn't, he'll have to step down—and live the rest of his life as a human."

Natalia's stomach dropped.

"But why?"

"Because the King or Queen of All That Is Magic can only live forever if they have a true partner to rule beside them—a bond of *real*, unbreakable love. Otherwise, their power fades."

Natalia felt sick.

"And if he can't?"

"No one knows," Siberanna said quietly, turning toward the window. "Magic itself chooses the next ruler... but since Jason Wolf is said to be the last human of pure goodness, we don't know what will happen if he's forced to step down."

Natalia said nothing—but her heart was heavy with guilt. *So if he loses his throne... it'll be my fault.*

Siberanna heard the thought and added softly, "Which is why we must find and defeat Campbell before that day comes."

CHAPTER 3

THE EVIL PLOT REVEALED

So many in the Magical Realm wanted Jason Wolf to remain king—and everyone wanted Campbell caught.

As Natalia and Siberanna continued their conversation about Campbell, neither of them realized that, in a dark and distant corner of the Magical Realm, Campbell and his minions, Gorman and Jeffgon, were watching everything unfold. They observed the scene through a large, square-shaped mirror that hung on a cave wall—one that appeared only when Campbell willed it.

This dark part of the realm was an underground cavern hidden beneath a small, shadowy forest, miles away from the place where they had escaped. Inside, there was barely any light. The only illumination came from a dim glow around an old, worn throne—upon which Campbell sat, watching the two girls' conversation, his two minions standing at either side.

After listening to Siberanna explain to Natalia what would happen if Jason were forced to step down, Gorman spoke up.

"Master, forgive me for saying this, but I think this girl—Natalia Summers—could become a real problem for you."

"And what makes you say that?" Campbell asked, his voice low and stern.

Jeffgon trembled before adding, "Well, Master, from what we can see, not only is this girl clever enough to help the king find us, but—"

"I doubt," Campbell interrupted, "that a girl like this has the ability to find us."

"All the same, Master!" Gorman pressed. "This human girl may or may not be the key to helping King Jason and others track us down—but it's clear she really likes the king. And you know what that could mean."

"I know what will happen, you idiots," Campbell said, shoving both Gorman and Jeffgon to the ground. "But you're forgetting something."

"Which is?" they both asked, scrambling back to their feet.

At that moment, Campbell waved his hand, and the mirror vanished. Just before it disappeared, he caught a final glimpse of Siberanna leaving Natalia in her room.

Turning to his minions, Campbell said, "That girl, Natalia, used to bully Jason before he ever learned about the Magical Realm or became king. She's also the reason he hasn't chosen anyone to be his queen. So why should we believe she's the one he would choose to rule by his side for eternity?"

The question made a certain sense—until Jeffgon spoke up.

"But, Master," he began nervously, "as the chronicles say, when two humans hate each other at such a young age, they're often hiding the fact that—"

"Silence!" Campbell roared.

Both Gorman and Jeffgon fell silent immediately, too afraid to say another word.

After a few tense seconds, Campbell continued, "All the same, Jason has proven how clever he can be. He's not to be underestimated."

"Because of that trap we walked into," Jeffgon blurted out without thinking.

For a brief moment, he thought Campbell might strike him down—but instead, Campbell sneered.

"Yes, you simple-minded fool. Because of that celebration trap he lured us into, I know it won't be long before he finds us."

"But, Master!" Gorman said in a trembling voice. "Many of the kings and queens before him never found us. Hardly anyone in the Magical Realm even comes to this area, so—"

"That's because," Campbell interrupted sharply, "none of those kings or queens ever came this close—or were this desperate—to have us captured."

He struck her across the face as he finished, laughing darkly as she cried out in pain.

Then, with a cruel grin, he added, "I don't plan to underestimate Jason again—not until this year comes to an end. Once he's forced to step down, and no one replaces him within a month and a half, I can finally launch my grand plan."

There was a moment of silence after he finished, until Jeffgon asked, "What is your plan again, Master?"

Campbell drew a wand from a small pocket in his robes and zapped both of them against a wall.

Then, with vicious sarcasm, he said, "What is my plan? What is my plan? Are you two really as dumb as humans?"

No one answered as Campbell sat back on his small throne.

"Well, I suppose that means I need to repeat myself — and I hate repeating myself where you two are concerned. Nevertheless, and this better be the last time I say it. My plan happens at the end of the year, when Jason Wolf is forced to step down as king. We all know he will have no choice—he'll never find a queen in time."

"I thought you were talking about your plan, Master," Jeffgon blurted, without thinking. "Not about how long the king has until he's forced to step down."

"I'm getting to that." Campbell zapped Jeffgon to the ground.

After Jeffgon had picked himself up, Campbell continued, "Now, where was I?" He paused for a few seconds. "Oh yes — when Jason Wolf is finally out of the way, my spell will take effect. Then the Magical Realm—and the Human Realm—will be mine."

"A wonderful plan, Master!" Gorman said, a wicked smile on her face.

After Jeffgon agreed that it was an ingenious plan, Campbell continued, "And it will work—as long as we aren't captured. That's why we'll find a hideout in the Human Realm."

Both minions stared at him in shock. Gorman finally spoke. "Master, are you sure that's a good idea?"

Campbell looked as though he might explode but managed to answer through clenched teeth.

"Yes, you fools. It's the last place they'll expect us to go. And even if they do try to find us there, they'll expose themselves long before they come close."

At last, both minions nodded, agreeing that it was, indeed, a good idea. They immediately began searching for a suitable hiding place in the Human Realm. As they worked, Campbell summoned the mirror once more. It showed Natalia sleeping peacefully in her bedroom. He stared at her for a long moment before making the mirror vanish again.

"It might be wise to keep an eye on you too, my dear," he murmured, "just in case you are the key to my downfall."

He paused, deep in thought, then added, "And I can't let Jason fool me again—not when I'm this close to ruling this world... and so many others."

Just as Campbell imagined all this and more, far away in the Human Realm—at exactly one o'clock in the morning—Natalia woke with a start. She had just experienced two dreams, but it was the second that made her bolt upright.

She wanted to go back to sleep, but she couldn't—especially as she whispered to herself, "I wonder if that good dream could ever come true. I'll think about that later. What scares me more is that dream about Campbell. Maybe I should tell Jason... or someone."

As these thoughts circled in her mind, Natalia realized she was thirsty and needed a drink to clear her head. She got out of bed, opened her bedroom door, and stepped into a grand hallway—long, wide, and gleaming marble white, with many doors painted in different colors. A magnificent ruby-red carpet stretched from one end to the other, glowing softly in the moonlight.

Natalia walked down the hall toward the kitchen. The house was large enough to get lost in, but she knew her way well enough—especially when she needed something in the middle of the night.

Just as she reached the top of the stairs, she heard her parents' voices. Their bedroom was right beside the stairwell, and as she passed their door, she couldn't help but overhear their conversation.

"I can't believe this is happening to us," her mother said softly.

"Well, believe it," her father replied, his voice sharp and cold—like that of a ruthless businessman. "Because of how much our daughter has cost us, and the fact that both of our companies are about to go bankrupt, we'll soon be forced to live like..."

He trailed off, unable to say the word, then continued with something far more cruel.

In fact, what he said was so insulting that it's the kind of thing upper-class people say when they enjoy looking down on the rest of us. Just another reason they are truly terrible people.

They believed people should work endless hours and days and have no lives of their own. They think they're the only ones entitled to live freely, while the rest of us exist merely to serve them. Another reason why the upper class deserves no respect in these dark times we live in.

As Natalia listened to her parents, she couldn't believe what she was hearing—especially when her mother said, in a sad, trembling voice, "Should we tell her?"

"No!" her father snapped.

From the sound of it, he was pacing up and down the room—near the door, too.

"We still have time. And hopefully, by the time things are as bad as we fear, Natalia will be eighteen—old enough to fend for herself."

"Do you really mean that?"

There was a long moment of silence after Natalia heard her mother say this. Even though she couldn't see it, her father felt ashamed of what he had said.

Still, in a calmer voice, he went on, "I just hate what our daughter has become. She always gets away with everything, and no one ever says a word. And after what Mr. and Mrs. Wolf—who were once my greatest friends—did, it's clear they no longer care who we are."

"Because unlike many people, they don't see the rich as bad," Natalia's mother replied softly.

Her father sighed.

"Can you blame anyone for thinking that way, after everything the president has done? After how many suffered during the crisis of his first term?"

"I know," she said quietly, regret in her voice.

"But as I was saying," he continued, "because of how our daughter treated their son, he ran away— and they haven't spoken to me since."

There was another heavy silence before Natalia's mother asked, "They still haven't found his secret home?"

"They gave up months ago," her father said. "It's as if the boy doesn't even exist anymore. Maybe if our daughter hadn't been such a bully to him, he might still be around."

Natalia almost cried when she heard that—but deep down, she knew her parents were wrong about some things.

A moment later, she heard her mother say, "Maybe if we'd been around more—and hadn't spoiled her so badly—she might be a different person."

"That doesn't change the fact," Natalia's father replied, "that because of all this, we might end up in the poorhouse—or worse, working middle-class jobs."

"You can't blame her for everything," her mother said gently.

"Well, maybe," her father said, his anger rising, "if she didn't see life as one big game or endless party—and actually learned how hard it can be out there—maybe, just maybe, she'd be a better person."

Natalia couldn't take it anymore. She turned and quietly made her way down to the kitchen.

As she descended the spiral staircase, she whispered to herself, "They're right about one thing. Maybe if I hadn't been such a spoiled brat, they wouldn't be in this much trouble."

She paused at the bottom of the stairs and stepped into a magnificent kitchen.

Sitting down at the table with a large glass of juice, she sighed and murmured, "Well, I guess it's too late to prove I can change... but maybe it's not too late to make sure they don't lose everything because of me."

After pouring herself a second glass of juice, Natalia sat for a while, deep in thought, wondering what she could possibly do to help. But no ideas came. She knew finding a job would be difficult—

especially with the country still reeling from all the trouble caused by the recent president, whose actions had done so much damage.

When she finally finished her drink, she placed the glass in the sink and quietly made her way back to bed. As she passed her parents' bedroom, she noticed their conversation had shifted. Then she heard her name and stopped to listen.

"I guess it's for the best, if it's our only option," her mother was saying.

"Well," her father replied in a calm voice, "we both know she'll never get her act together—but this school might be good for her."

There was a moment of silence before her mother spoke again.

"But will we be able to afford it after we go bankrupt?"

"She only needs one year," her father said. "That should be enough—and with luck, the school might even keep her a few more years after that."

Natalia went back to her room, distraught by what she had heard.

Turning off the lights, she whispered to herself, "I'm not going to finishing school."

She knew exactly which school they were talking about.

"But I do know where I'm going," she murmured. "I just hope he'll be okay with it when I ask."

CHAPTER 4

PLANS

The next day, Natalia was taken to the Palace of the Magical Realm by the wizard Moongum. She had been awakened before sunrise, which meant she hadn't gotten much sleep—but she didn't really care. It had been impossible to rest after hearing what her parents had said the night before.

As they traveled, Natalia couldn't help but wonder what would happen when they arrived at the palace—and what the king would say when she told him about her dream. She only hoped he would believe her.

When they appeared in the palace's throne room, Natalia saw that Jason was speaking with a large group of magical creatures—most of them warriors and soldiers, judging by their armor and serious expressions.

Natalia was awestruck by the beauty of the throne room. It was a vast, square chamber with gleaming ruby-red stone walls and a smooth blue ceiling adorned with three skylights placed side by side. The floor was made of polished gold, with a grand carpet of gold and diamond stripes leading from the towering silver double doors at the entrance all the way to the throne itself.

Beyond those doors stretched a magnificent hallway and an enormous balcony that overlooked the kingdom. At the far end of the carpet sat the throne—the very same one Jason had occupied the night before, when Natalia and her friends had discovered his secret, and when Campbell and his minions had narrowly escaped the trap that had been set for them.

When Jason saw that everyone had gathered, he rose and said in a regal voice, "Everyone, I would like to say that I've been doing a lot of thinking since last night's events, and—"

"Sire!" Siberanna interrupted from behind Natalia. "You're not going to say what we think you're going to say. We can't give up."

Jason didn't seem angered by her interruption, but he gave her an uneasy look and said, "By now, he's probably left his hideout. I can't help but wish we'd taken the fight to him instead of waiting for him to come to us."

"Sire," Moongum began in a gentle, fatherly tone, "you know as well as everyone in this realm that no one dares to enter that region—not even your strongest and bravest warriors."

Jason nodded in agreement and was about to respond when Natalia suddenly spoke up.

"I think I might know where he is now."

The moment she said it, the entire room fell silent. Everyone—including Jason—turned to her in surprise.

Rising from his throne, Jason asked, "What are you talking about?"

It took Natalia a moment to speak—she felt uneasy with everyone staring at her—but when she finally gathered her courage, she said, "I had a dream about him, Sire."

"A dream?" Jason repeated, his voice stern.

Then, turning to the others in the room, he asked, "What does she mean by that?"

Moongum stepped forward and replied in a kind but cautious tone, "Well, Sire, it is said that some dreams from humans, especially nightmares, can be connected to this realm."

"In that case," Jason said, turning toward a group of witches, "extract the dream from her mind and show it to me at once."

Before the witches could begin their spell, Natalia asked nervously, "It's not going to hurt me, is it?"

The witches laughed softly, and one of them said, "It's a simple spell, dear. You won't feel a thing."

Natalia stayed perfectly still as the witches chanted their spell. Then something extraordinary happened—a small, shimmering screen appeared above her head, displaying her memories and dreams for everyone in the throne room to see.

The witches hastened the vision, fast-forwarding through her memories until they reached the part they were looking for.

At last, when the right moment appeared, Jason raised his hand and said sharply, "Stop—right there!"

It was a good thing Jason had stopped them when he did—because what they were seeing was the inside of Campbell's hideout, something no one had ever thought possible. They watched Campbell talking to his minions about his plan to ruin Jason.

At first, everyone thought it was a waste of time. Campbell was only repeating what they thought they already knew; but when the vision reached its end, Jason asked the witches to lift their spell from Natalia.

He explained aloud, "He plans to hide in the Human Realm, believing we won't find him there."

"He can't be serious, can he?" Siberanna exclaimed.

"What are you talking about?" Natalia asked, confused.

Siberanna chuckled softly.

"Well, Natalia, you're new to all this, so I wouldn't expect you to understand."

"Try me," Natalia said firmly.

Siberanna raised an eyebrow, surprised but impressed by her boldness.

"Very well," she said at last. "I will."

Siberanna took a deep breath and said, "You see, no magical creature in their right mind would ever think that hiding in the Human Realm is a good idea."

Natalia laughed and replied, "Well, whoever said he *was* in his right mind?"

Her comment made everyone burst into laughter.

"You have a point there," Siberanna said, still trying to stop laughing.

When the laughter finally subsided, the king spoke.

"He probably believes we'd never expect him to go there."

A long silence followed until a large female troll stepped forward.

"Sire," she said, "would you like me to send some of my best troops into that realm to find and capture him?"

Jason hesitated.

"Are you sure that's a good idea, Captain?" he asked uneasily.

"Of course, Your Majesty," the troll replied confidently.

Jason opened his mouth to respond, but the troll captain spoke first.

"No need to worry, my king," she said confidently. "My troops are masters of disguise and know how to outsmart humans—which is exactly what we'll need to do if we're to find Campbell and his minions."

The king nodded in agreement, just as Natalia asked, "What does she mean by that?"

Jason chuckled softly before explaining, "Campbell has a dark gift—he can spread fear and shadow into the hearts of those too weak to resist it. If he's hiding in the Human Realm, many humans will fall under that magic's influence."

"Which will make it easier for us to find him," the troll captain added.

"Perhaps," Jason said thoughtfully, "but it also means he'll likely avoid large human settlements."

"All the same, Your Majesty," the troll captain replied firmly, "we'll find him—and when we do, he'll no longer be a threat to you or to the Magical Realm."

"Just keep me informed at all times," Jason ordered.

"I will, Your Majesty," she said with a respectful bow.

"And I think," Natalia began in a steady, determined voice, "I know a few places he's likely to go."

Everyone turned to her as she described several locations that most humans avoided—old houses rumored to be haunted, deep shadowy woods, and long-forgotten dump sites. She even mentioned a few isolated islands considered too dangerous to visit. When they asked for more, she simply shook her head and said that was all she knew.

"Well, everyone," said the king, deciding he'd heard enough, "we'd better start planning where to begin our search. And, Natalia—" he paused, almost smiling, "I can't believe I'm saying this, but thank you for everything you're doing for us."

Natalia blushed and smiled. "Thank you, Your Majesty. But all I'm trying to do is show how sorry I am for everything I did to you—and prove that I can become a better person."

Everyone seemed moved by her words. The king, however, spoke in a more cautious tone.

"Well, Natalia, I still haven't given much thought to forgiving you for the trouble you caused me in the past—or for what could have happened if you'd gone through with what you wanted."

"I understand, Sire," she said softly, lowering her gaze to the floor.

Her humility made Jason's expression soften.

"But," he added after a moment, "after the help you've given us today, I'm starting to think about it. Still, our past isn't something that's easy to forget."

"I understand," she said.

A few seconds later, a small goblin stepped forward and asked if they could leave. The king gave a nod of approval, and the great double doors swung open, allowing many to exit the throne room.

As the king watched people file out to the right and left through the grand hallway, his gaze drifted toward the large balcony window. Just as he was about to rise from his throne and leave the room himself, he noticed Natalia standing by the window, staring outside. Curious, he walked over to her.

"Enjoying the view?" he asked.

She jumped slightly at the sound of his voice, then turned to him after a moment and said, "I just couldn't help but notice—you have a wonderful kingdom. It's far more beautiful than anything we see in Northburg."

Jason chuckled softly at that. For a few moments, they both stood in silence, gazing out at the scenery.

Then he said, "The Magical Realm truly is a remarkable place—and I'm proud to be the one responsible for it."

"And you do a great job, from what I hear," Natalia said with a small smile.

"Thanks," he said, feeling a bit embarrassed.

The view before them was truly breathtaking. Below lay villages that looked as though they belonged to the Middle Ages—stone cottages, cobbled streets, and curling wisps of chimney smoke rising into the clear blue sky. Beyond them flowed fresh, sparkling rivers bordered by rows of tall, green trees. Near the horizon stretched wide, rolling fields of emerald grass and distant mountains where dragons and griffins soared gracefully through the air.

In the villages below, children laughed and played beneath the sun on what could only be described as the most beautiful summer day imaginable.

As the king slowly drew his attention back to the present, he noticed tears glistening in Natalia's eyes.

He handed her a small cloth to wipe them away and asked gently, "Are you okay?"

"I really don't want to talk about it," she said softly, blowing her nose.

Jason was about to turn and walk away when Natalia suddenly added, "My parents don't want me to live with them anymore."

"What?" he asked, startled.

She went on to tell him everything she had overheard her parents saying the night before. As she spoke, Jason felt a deep sympathy for her growing inside him.

When she finally finished, he said, "So they think the only way to get you to change is to send you to finishing school?"

Natalia nodded.

"I feel awful that they're going bankrupt—and terrible for all the trouble I've caused them. But this..."

Her voice trailed off into silence.

Then, in a quiet, almost hopeless tone, she turned to Jason and said, "I know I have no right to ask you this, but... is there somewhere here in this realm I could stay? Because—"

"There's no place in the Magical Realm where you can stay," he said, a sad expression crossing his face. "But if you follow me, I'll take you to a room in the palace I think you might like."

Natalia was stunned.

"Wait—after everything—?"

"In the past," he interrupted gently, "I never would have done something like this for you. But after everything you've done to help us, you deserve to call this palace—and this realm—your home."

Natalia was deeply grateful, though she couldn't help feeling it was too much kindness.

When she tried to protest, the king simply asked, "Would you rather your parents send you to finishing school?"

When she quickly said no, he nodded toward the hallway.

"Then follow me."

Together, they walked down into a part of the palace Natalia had never seen before.

Meanwhile, in another part of the palace, Siberanna, Moongum, and a few others gathered secretly in a small, square-shaped room. For a moment, no one spoke. Then Moongum broke the silence.

"Has anyone besides me noticed why Natalia's attitude toward the king has changed?"

Everyone had expected him to bring this up.

"That's because, after seeing what he can do—" Siberanna began.

"But according to the *Chronicle of Ancient Magic*," Moongum interrupted with a knowing smile.

The *Chronicle of Ancient Magic*, which Moongum often referenced, was a legendary scroll of knowledge said to contain details about every living being across all worlds, along with their complete histories.

Before Moongum could continue, Siberanna cut in, her voice edged with concern.

"Moongum, is that all you ever talk about? Because I really don't like how convinced you are that Natalia is the one meant to marry the king—and spend eternity with him."

Moongum gave her an uneasy look.

"It's not the only thing I talk about," he said calmly. "But I'm only trying to make sure the last known human of pure good remains king forever."

"Do you think I'm not trying too?" Siberanna shot back, her tone rising with frustration. "I know Natalia is changing—becoming a better person—but that doesn't change the fact that she's stopped us from finding him a queen to rule beside him."

There was a long silence before Siberanna spoke again.

"But, on the other hand," she said thoughtfully, "Natalia truly is our only hope if we want the king to continue ruling. And in the throne room earlier, I thought I sensed... a spark between them."

"Even Campbell," said a gremlin from the shadows, "believes Natalia could destroy his plans—if she and the king were to fall in love."

"This means we need to find a way to bring those two together!" declared a male werewolf.

Another silence followed as everyone in the room exchanged uncertain glances, waiting for someone else to speak.

At last, Siberanna said, her voice uncertain, "As much as I agree this is a bold plan to stop Campbell and his minions once and for all, the question remains—how do we get two people who've hated each other for so long to not only fall in love, but become the permanent rulers of the entire Magical Realm?"

"I think we'll find a few ways around that," Moongum said.

At his words, Siberanna—who still felt uneasy about the idea of forcing such a thing—opened her mouth to respond, but a vampire cut her off.

"Do you really want our realm to fall into the Dark Age?" he hissed. "Because that's exactly what will happen if Campbell wins."

Siberanna felt her anger rising, but she also knew he was right. She couldn't allow the Magical Realm to fall into darkness.

Taking a deep breath, she said, "All right, then. How do we get those two to fall in love?"

As this was happening, Jason and Natalia reached another part of the palace and stopped in front of a pair of grand double doors made of silver wood.

Placing a hand on one of the handles, Jason said, "Here we are."

Before Natalia could respond, he pushed the doors open—and to her astonishment, revealed a magnificent bedroom, so breathtaking it had to be seen to be believed.

As they stepped inside, Jason said cheerfully, "Well? Any chance this will do?"

For a moment, Natalia was too amazed to speak.

Then, with pure joy in her voice, she said, "This is the most beautiful bedroom I've ever seen! But... you're serious? It's really mine?"

"It is," he said with a smile. "But this isn't even the best part."

"You mean there's more?" Natalia asked, her eyes wide as she looked around the room.

The bedroom was enormous—at least ten times larger than an ordinary one. On the left stood a grand bed of equal size, with elegant drawers on either side. To the right was a luxurious bathroom, twice as large as any normal one, filled with everything she could possibly imagine. The bedroom also had a small table with a large mirror at the far end, but what truly caught Natalia's eye were the great, colorless curtains.

In fact, the entire room seemed colorless— muted yet elegant. When Jason waved his hand, the curtains drew back on their own, revealing a wide balcony that reminded Natalia of the one near the throne room. But this one had something even more breathtaking—a grand view of the ocean.

Overcome with excitement, Natalia ran straight toward the balcony's edge and nearly lost her balance—but caught herself just in time. She stood there, gazing out at the endless waves and breathing in the crisp, salty air.

As Jason joined her, he said softly, "This is the Enchanted Ocean."

Before them stretched the clearest, most beautiful sea imaginable—its surface shimmering with light and color, like glass beneath the sun. Natalia's eyes moved over every inch of it in awe.

"This ocean," Jason continued, "is home to most of my water people, but..."

He trailed off, deciding not to spoil the moment. For a brief second, he wondered why he was letting himself get so caught up in it—and whether Natalia might one day take advantage of his kindness. After all, she had a history of doing just that.

"Are you okay?" she asked, watching him closely.

"I'm fine," he said quickly.

But Natalia could tell he wasn't being honest— she could almost read what was on his mind. Before she could say anything, a few merpeople leapt gracefully out of the water, splashing back down before calling out to their king.

"Good day, Your Majesty!"

"Good day to you, too," Jason replied with a small smile.

When they had gone, Natalia turned to him and said quietly, "I know what's on your mind."

He looked at her in surprise.

"What do you mean?"

"Well," she began, "I know I used to take advantage of things—of people—just to get what I wanted. But not anymore. I really wish you could see that."

A heavy silence fell between them as Jason turned his gaze back to the ocean.

"I'm trying," he said at last, his voice low. "Really, I am—but—"

"But it's just hard to believe in something that feels impossible to see," Natalia added.

Jason smiled.

"Exactly. And how did you know I was going to say that?"

"Moongum told me," she said, sounding a bit uneasy. "When he brought me here, he also said you never thought you'd see the day I'd turn over a new leaf. Which—I don't blame you for, because..."

She trailed off, afraid she had said too much.

Jason knew that when someone had been bullied their whole life, and the person who hurt them tries to change, it just might be worth giving them the chance to prove they're not the same anymore. No matter how painful the past was, sometimes people can show how sorry they are— without ever saying the words.

When Jason led Natalia back into her new room, he said, "I know you might not like the color, but you can change it to whatever you want."

"How?" she asked, her tone sharp with curiosity.

"Just say it—and think of the color you want it to be."

Natalia closed her eyes for a few seconds, and when she opened them, she gasped. The walls had turned a deep, rich purple. Her blankets, pillows, and sheets were now light red, and even the bed itself had changed to a darker shade of crimson. The floor and ceiling shimmered with a soft blue glow.

Looking around in wonder, she whispered, "What just happened?"

Jason chuckled.

"That's the magic of the bedrooms here in the Magical Realm," he said. "You can make them look any way you like. And if you close your eyes again and think about all the things you left behind in the—"

He didn't have to finish. In that instant, everything Natalia owned appeared in her new room—each item perfectly placed, as though she had arranged it herself.

When she noticed another door beside the bathroom, she asked where it led. Jason smiled.

"That's your new walk-in closet."

Natalia gasped and ran straight to the door. It swung open on its own, revealing something that left her speechless. The moment she stepped inside, she saw rows of beautiful garments—more clothes than she had ever owned, and several styles she had never even seen before.

"Those are called robes," Jason explained. "They're the fashion of this realm, but if—"

"Oh no," she interrupted quickly. "I love them! But... why am I getting them?"

Jason chuckled softly before saying, "I think you already know the answer to that."

Natalia beamed with happiness. She stepped toward him, gave him a warm hug, and—without thinking—kissed him on the cheek.

The moment it happened, Jason felt something stir inside him—something he had to force himself to ignore. Still, he found himself hugging her back. In that instant, confusion set in. He didn't understand why he was doing it, or why he suddenly didn't want to let go.

Just as something seemed about to happen between them, the door opened and Siberanna entered. When she saw them, she froze—and immediately wished she hadn't.

"I hope I'm not interrupting anything," she said carefully.

Jason quickly stepped back from Natalia and replied, "Not at all. What is it, Siberanna?"

"Well, Sire," Siberanna began, still hating herself for having walked in at the wrong moment, "the Lord of Spellcaster City is here to see you."

Jason sighed and pressed a hand to his forehead.

"Very well. I'll see what he wants *this* time."

Before leaving, he turned back to Natalia.

"Would you like me to stay?"

"Oh no, Sire," she said quickly. "I think I can finish settling in. But if Siberanna wants to stay so I have someone to talk to, I don't mind."

Siberanna blinked, confused at first, then looked around the room.

In a voice that was half-pleased, half-uneasy, she asked, "Your Majesty... is she *living* here now?"

"Yes, she is," Jason replied simply.

Then he explained Natalia's situation to her.

As he spoke, Siberanna's eyes widened. She placed a hand over her heart, her mouth falling open in disbelief.

"And since she wants to help us capture Campbell and his minions—"

"I think I understand, Sire," Siberanna interrupted, though Jason didn't seem to mind. "And I think it's a good idea. It's very noble of you to show her such kindness."

Jason opened his mouth to respond but stopped himself. He was already running late. As he headed for the door, he said, "I'd like to talk more, but I'd better see what the Lord of Spellcaster City wants first. It had better not be the same as last time... I already warned him what would happen if he complained about that again."

"What do you mean?" Natalia asked, curious.

Jason paused at the doorway, glanced back, and said with a faint smile, "Trust me—you don't want to know."

Before Natalia could say another word, he was gone—leaving the two girls alone in the room.

As Natalia began arranging a few of her things in their new places, Siberanna spoke gently.

"I'm sorry your family is going bankrupt."

Natalia didn't respond right away.

After a moment, she sat down on a couch and said, "I always knew it would happen eventually.

And I know I wasn't any better with them than I was with the king. But if they think they're better off without me, so be it. I just hope I can be more useful here than I ever was in the Human Realm."

"You don't really mean that," Siberanna said softly, feeling sorry for her.

"I do!" Natalia said quickly, cutting her off. "At least I don't have to worry about finishing school now."

Both girls laughed, and Siberanna added, "I've heard that's a place hardly anyone in the Human Realm enjoys going to."

"That's true," Natalia agreed with a small smile.

After a few moments of comfortable silence, Siberanna said, "It was kind of His Majesty to do this for you."

"And I am grateful for it," Natalia said quickly, before she could stop herself—she'd had enough of hearing about it. "I just wish I'd changed a long time ago. Still, I can't help feeling that this is too much kindness from the king... something I don't really deserve."

"And that's exactly what's making all of us—including the king—see that you *do* deserve it," Siberanna replied. "But I hope you're not planning to expect that kind of kindness all the time."

Natalia gave her a firm look.

"This is enough for me. All I want now is to help find and capture Campbell and his two minions."

"And we *will* get him," Siberanna said as she stood, preparing to leave.

"I'd just like to know where to go if I want something to eat," Natalia said.

"You don't have to go anywhere," Siberanna replied with a laugh. "Just say what you want, and it'll appear right in front of you."

Natalia stood from the couch, intrigued.

"Are you saying if I want a sub with—"

She didn't get to finish. The moment she started speaking, a ruby-red platter appeared in her hands, holding a perfectly made sub—loaded with everything she liked.

As she sat back down, Siberanna grinned.

"How's that for magic?"

Natalia didn't answer right away as she was already taking a big bite.

When she finally swallowed, she said with a smile, "That's really cool—and definitely something to get used to."

Siberanna smiled warmly, then said, "Before I go, there's something I'd like to ask you."

Natalia felt a knot of worry, but said, "Go ahead."

"Well," Siberanna said, "many of us have noticed you seem happier—and a little nervous—around the king. I just wanted to know if there's a reason for it."

It took Natalia a moment to reply. She walked to the bed, sat first, then said quietly, "I don't really know. It's like a strange feeling overtakes me when I'm near him."

Siberanna smiled.

"I think you'll understand in time. I have to go now but enjoy your new home—and feel free to explore the palace. I mean anywhere."

After she left, Natalia climbed into her new bed and drifted off for a short, happy nap.

Unfortunately, something was about to spoil it. Unseen by anyone in the room, a small dark cloud hovered nearby — a portal that allowed Campbell to watch. He and his two minions were hidden in a large sewer beneath a city called Boston.

Campbell scowled when he saw the moment between Jason and Natalia.

He dismissed his minions and sat back on his small throne, his voice low and creepy as he muttered, "So this girl is a threat to my plans? I'll have to do something about that."

He began to scheme. The only way, he decided, to stop them from becoming a couple would be to kidnap her. But how could he do it without risking capture himself?

CHAPTER 5
DUTIES OF THE KING

It took some time for Natalia to get used to living not only in the Magical Realm but in the palace itself. On her second day there, she sent a text to her parents, telling them she overheard everything they'd said—and that they no longer needed to worry about her, since she was out of their lives for good. Instead of trying to bring her back, her parents simply accepted it.

Their quick acceptance of her message, made her realize that parents who believe they're better off without their children are the ones who shouldn't be parents at all. After all, there's nothing greater—or harder—than doing what's truly best for one's child. If they wanted to have children so badly, how could they not have been ready for her, or the future that followed?

Natalia quickly began to enjoy palace life. She attended school from time to time through the portal, sometimes with Jason and sometimes on her own. She usually went alone, since Jason's duties kept him in the Magical Realm.

Not long after, Natalia learned through another dream that Campbell and his minions were hiding in Boston. A strong team of soldiers was sent there through a portal to locate him without alerting him to their presence. That proved to be the hard part, Natalia noticed when she saw the situation firsthand.

They eventually found a way to keep Campbell contained without him realizing it. Still, when a few soldiers warned Natalia that he might try to capture her, they insisted she needed protection. Because of that, she had to miss school almost every day and spent most of her time wandering the palace to pass the hours.

Natalia enjoyed exploring—every hallway, every chamber, every hidden staircase. The palace was enormous, almost impossible to describe from the outside, and she often wondered how anyone managed to reach every part of it in a single day.

More than anything, though, Natalia looked for excuses to spend time with Jason—and he didn't seem to mind. In fact, it made him happy. Many who needed to speak with him began to postpone their meetings or reschedule entirely, often saying whatever they had to discuss could wait.

Jason didn't realize it, but most of those around him were secretly hoping something good would happen between the two of them—and soon, before it was too late.

As time went on, Natalia began to understand why Jason was rarely seen in the Human Realm. Being king wasn't an easy job—a fact she quickly learned as she watched all that he did, day after day.

Most days, Jason was in meetings with lords, ladies, and land leaders from across the Magical Realm, discussing trade, resources, and ways to ensure everyone could make a living and thrive. Like the great rulers before him, Jason focused not on what he could gain, but on what he could *give*. He believed true leaders served their people—and that those who took from others for their own benefit weren't leaders at all, but tyrants and dictators.

Natalia was sometimes allowed to attend these meetings, and to everyone's surprise, she offered several clever ideas to help ensure fairness and balance across the realm. Her suggestions not only met people's needs but often exceeded their expectations.

Jason and the other leaders were impressed. At first, Jason suspected she might be trying to take his place, but that doubt vanished quickly when she finished by saying,

"I'm not trying to do your job, Your Majesty. I just want to help make things easier for you—and for everyone who depends on you."

Her words caught him off guard. For the first time, Jason saw in her not as the spoiled girl she once was, but someone truly willing to change. And as the others in the room nodded in approval, he couldn't help but smile, realizing just how much Natalia had grown since the day she arrived.

"I'm glad you like this," she said, "but I think the king should have the final say."

Her words made him smile. From that day on, he allowed her to attend many of his meetings, and through them, Natalia soon discovered that the Magical Realm and the Human Realm weren't the only worlds that existed.

There were other realms as well, each with their own rulers—and Jason was required to meet with those leaders at least once every other week.

In addition, he often had to address issues across the many villages and regions of the Magical Realm. Some problems he handled with ease, but there were times when he faced difficult decisions that upset his people at first.

In the end, though, his choices always proved to be for the greater good—like the time he had to intervene in one of the dwarven mines, where the workers were fighting over the claim to a large and mysterious ruby.

Jason tried everything he could to convince the dwarves to share the ruby, but in the end, he was forced to destroy it—shattering it into a million pieces.

One of the dwarves stared in disbelief and asked, "Sire... why?"

Natalia wondered the same thing.

"I'm not going to let you behave like humans—fighting over something so meaningless," the king said firmly.

The dwarves began to protest, but before they could, the shattered ruby glowed and multiplied, forming even larger gems. Amazed, the dwarves bowed and thanked the king, returning to their work—no longer fighting over something so foolish.

There were many other situations like this that Jason had to handle, and Natalia often helped him. She loved every moment of it.

Later, as they rode together in a flying carriage, Natalia said, "Wow... I never realized everything you go through."

"Well, Natalia," Jason replied with a weary smile, "these are my duties and my responsibilities. It's why I'm always so worn out."

"No wonder you're never at school much," she teased.

He chuckled.

"Well, as King, I have to stay calm—and only be tough when the situation demands it."

"Which I've seen plenty of," she said, smiling kindly.

Before she could say more, Jason added quietly, "Still... even though I have to act that way here, I sometimes wonder if I can be that strong when I really need to be."

"And that's why I'm helping you," she said softly, feeling a pang of guilt.

When he opened his mouth to respond, she continued, "Seeing everything you go through—everything you do for this world and its people—makes me wish—"

"Natalia," he interrupted gently, raising a hand for silence. "You've been an incredible help, and I'm truly glad to have you on my side. Honestly... I kind of like us being friends more than enemies."

She giggled. "I like it too—and I hope I've been a good friend."

Jason laughed.

"Like I just said, you've been a huge help—especially with how you handled so many of today's problems."

"Hey, all I did was spot the source and point it out," she said with a grin. "I didn't really think."

"Well, you did wonderfully," he said warmly. "And I'm very grateful for it."

This was the spark everyone in the Magical Realm had been hoping for. They wanted that spark to grow—because it's the kind of hope their world needed.

As time went by, Natalia began to feel exhausted from everything she'd been doing. One Saturday morning, she decided to sleep in—partly because she was tired, and partly because she adored her new bed. In fact, there were days she found it hard to get up at all, which was another reason she'd missed so much school. While she was sound asleep and lost in a wonderful dream, she suddenly felt someone shaking her awake.

At first, she was furious and ready to complain to the king—or anyone who would listen—but when she opened her eyes and saw who it was, her anger vanished.

With joy and laughter in her voice, she cried out, "Amanda! Samantha!"

After hugging her two best friends tightly, Amanda said with excitement, "We heard rumors that you were living in the palace!"

"You heard right," Natalia said happily. "And I've really enjoyed it here. But enough about me—how are you two doing?"

Amanda and Samantha exchanged a quick glance, then Amanda grinned and said, "Well... notice anything different about us?"

Looking at them more closely, Natalia noticed that Amanda's red hair and lips were a little darker than before, and her eyes gave off a faint flash every time she blinked. Her skin was noticeably paler, and she seemed stronger—her long, sharp fangs visible only when she spoke. She wore dark robes now and no longer looked entirely human.

As for Samantha, she was covered in thick black-and-brown wolf fur, complete with wolf ears, teeth, and even a tail. Her hands, feet, and face still looked human, and she could still walk upright, but her new form gave her a fierce, majestic presence. Like Amanda, she wore a well-crafted set of robes.

Natalia was delighted by her friends' new appearances.

Smiling, she said, "Well, I have to say, you two look better than ever—especially after what I saw at your last training sessions."

"You've been to our training sessions?" Amanda asked in surprise.

Before either of them could say more, Natalia replied, "Only on the days when the king had to attend, inspect and judge the final events."

"Why didn't you tell us you were there?" Samantha asked, scratching her head.

Natalia explained that because Amanda and Samantha were still in training, there was a risk they might lose control. After all, she and the king had seen that stage firsthand during their inspections, and none of their masters wanted to take unnecessary chances.

"And that's why I couldn't talk to you during those times, and—"

"We understand!" both girls said at once.

A brief silence followed as Amanda and Samantha looked curiously around the room.

After a few moments, Samantha turned to Natalia and asked, "So... how come you're living here now?"

Natalia got off the bed and walked into her closet as she began to answer. While getting dressed, she told them everything she'd overheard her parents say that night—how it had left her hurt and angry.

Both girls were furious on her behalf.

Then Natalia told them what happened when she shared the story with the king.

Emerging from the closet in a new set of elegant robes, she said, "At first, I thought that because of our past, he'd refuse to help me. But instead, he showed me to this room—and I was so grateful."

Both girls were stunned; but Natalia continued, walking toward the balcony and gazing out at the ocean.

"I know in the past I took advantage of so many people," she said softly, "but not anymore."

Both her friends smiled at that.

Then Amanda said, "You really are turning into a new person. But tell me—do you still like this room better than your old one?"

It took Natalia a moment to answer. She stood gazing out at the horizon before finally saying, "I do... but it's a shame it might not be for long."

Both her friends looked startled.

"What do you mean?" Amanda asked.

"Well," Natalia said quietly, "if the king doesn't find a queen before the year ends..."

"He'll be forced to step down," Samantha finished for her.

"And from what everyone's saying," Amanda added, "he might be the last king of this realm—and of All That Is Magic."

"How do you know about that?" Natalia asked, her voice full of confusion.

The two girls exchanged a look before Samantha said, "Our masters told us."

Amanda nodded and continued, "They also said that even if Campbell and his minions are captured, the idea of losing the best ruler this realm has ever had is just... too sad to imagine."

Natalia fell silent, lost in thought. Memories came rushing back—of all the times Jason had nearly found someone special in the Human Realm, and of how she had ruined every chance he had. If she hadn't, the Magical Realm wouldn't now be facing such a terrible fate.

"You okay?" Amanda and Samantha asked at once, their voices full of concern.

It took Natalia a moment to find her words, but when she finally shared what was on her mind, Amanda said, "This is something I never thought I'd say—but I'm going to anyway. Those girls he tried to charm didn't deserve a man like King Jason Wolf."

"Amanda's right," Samantha added. "None of them would've brought him the kind of happiness he deserves for the rest of his life."

Natalia chuckled softly.

When her friends asked what was so funny, she replied, "That's just it—it has to be true, unbreakable love when he finds his queen, or it doesn't count. If he *does* find her, and stays on as king of this realm, he'll get to live forever—just like you two."

Amanda and Samantha exchanged startled looks.

With a hint of laughter in her voice, Natalia said, "Wait—you mean you two didn't know that by becoming citizens of this realm, you'll live forever?"

There was a moment of silence before they explained they hadn't gotten that far yet in their training.

"We're still learning," Amanda said. "How to balance and control the beast within—and to embrace it as part of who we are."

Natalia instantly wished she hadn't said anything. If their masters' hadn't told them yet, she wondered what might happen if they found out another way.

"Oh, don't be sorry," Amanda said with a grin. "It just means our masters have one less thing to tell us."

All three girls laughed, then turned back to gaze out over the ocean. After a few quiet moments, Amanda spoke again in a teasing tone.

"So, Natalia... tell us more. Since you've been spending so much time with the king, or Jason Wolf, as we used to know him, there've been *rumors* going around."

"What kind of rumors?" Natalia asked, her voice uneasy.

She wasn't sure she wanted to know.

Neither of them answered right away. They hesitated, unsure if she was ready to hear it. But when Natalia pressed again, they finally told her what people had been saying ever since she came to live in the palace.

~~~~~

In the throne room, King Jason sat reading a long scroll—and growing increasingly frustrated. Still, he pressed on, hoping to find what he was
~~~~~

looking for. He had been studying the scroll since the night before, and the reason for his frustration was simple: it was the *Chronicle* itself.

He was searching for a loophole—some ancient clause or hidden truth—that might allow him to remain king without a queen by his side. But no matter how long he searched, or how many lines he reread, there was nothing that could help him.

Just when he thought he'd found something, Siberanna appeared out of nowhere and said in a bright, cheerful voice, "Good morning, Your Majesty."

Jason didn't respond.

But when she noticed what he was reading, her expression changed, and she asked sharply, "Sire, why are you reading *that*?"

This time, he did answer.

"I was just seeing if I could find anything that might help me capture Campbell and his two fools—and maybe a loophole that would let me stay on as king without needing a queen by my side."

Silence filled the room.

Then Siberanna stepped closer and said quietly, "You really don't want to step down, do you, Sire?"

"I don't," the king said firmly. "Because unlike many before me, I have nothing to return to in the Human Realm. And if I step down... I won't get to live forever."

"Still," Siberanna said gently, "not everyone before you wanted what you want, Your Majesty."

Jason fell silent again, searching for the right words.

At last, he said softly, "I just don't want to die—especially after seeing what happens to most humans when they do."

They both laughed at that, and then Siberanna said, "You know, Sire, since you've been spending so much time with Natalia, everyone's starting to think—"

"Please don't finish that sentence, Siberanna," the king interrupted.

"Forgive me, Your Majesty!" she said quickly, stepping back. "It's just—"

"Yes, I know about the rumors," the king said before she could continue. "They're already making me regret letting her live here—or bringing her along to so many meetings, events, and celebrations... even when I'm handling matters of this realm."

"Well, Sire," Siberanna began carefully, choosing her words. "Many people have noticed how well you and Natalia get along—and the way you both look at each other. Maybe just—"

"I know what you're trying to do, Siberanna," he interrupted. "But because of our history, I don't want to go any further than friendship. Even if it *did* work, I don't think she could handle a life like this... not for all eternity."

That was exactly the hint Siberanna had been hoping for. She knew there was something she could work with.

Still, when she excused herself, she left the throne room quietly, leaving the king alone.

Jason sighed and muttered to himself, "Why am I being so stupid?"

The moment Siberanna stepped out of the throne room and into the palace hallway, she ran into Natalia.

As she passed by, noticing the girl gazing out one of the tall front windows, she asked, "What are you doing down here?"

Natalia jumped at the sound of her voice.

"Nothing," she said quickly.

Siberanna noticed the faint shimmer of tears in her eyes.

"Are you okay?" she asked gently.

Natalia didn't respond, but as a witch, Siberanna could sense what was troubling her.

Hoping to help, she said, "How much did you overhear from my conversation with the king?"

Natalia's eyes widened.

"How did you know I was eavesdropping?"

Siberanna smiled faintly.

"It's a witch thing. Now—how much did you hear?"

It took Natalia a moment to answer.

As the two of them started down a long staircase made of red stone, she finally said, feeling uneasy, "Well... after the talk I had with my two best friends, I started to realize that maybe what Moongum said that night—and the rumors I've been hearing about me and the king—might actually be true. Maybe I *do* like him... more than as a friend. Maybe I even *love* him."

Those were the very words Siberanna had been hoping to hear.

But, knowing Natalia's history, she couldn't help asking, "Do you really mean that, or—"

"Yes, I mean it," Natalia said sharply. "And I know what you were about to say, but this is different. These feelings—I think I've had them for a long time. I was just too stupid to realize it until now."

"And after hearing what the king said," Siberanna added softly, feeling a little sad herself, "it's making me see things differently."

Natalia spoke in a low, sorrowful voice.

"If you hadn't gone into the throne room before I did, I never would've gone in there and embarrassed myself."

A brief silence followed before she continued, "Now I almost wish I'd never discovered his secret... maybe things would've been better that way."

"Oh, don't say that!" Siberanna said, trying to cheer her up as they reached the bottom of the stairs. "From the sound of it, you didn't hear everything."

She waited for Natalia to respond, but when she didn't, Siberanna went on, "He's afraid you might not be able to accept this kind of life—and given your past, he worries it might be too much for you right now."

Her words didn't help. In fact, they only made Natalia feel even sadder.

Siberanna smiled kindly and said, "Just give it some time. Maybe—just maybe—things will change for the better, as they've been doing ever since you came here."

The next few days that followed were stressful for the king and for many others in the Magical Realm. Countless events demanded his presence, leaving him with little rest or time to himself. The only upside was that he got to miss school in the Human Realm—but even then, there were moments when he almost wished he were back in class instead of dealing with royal duties.

Natalia, on the other hand, enjoyed these events. She thought they were far grander than anything she had ever experienced before.

One of the events she witnessed was dragon fighting—something like bullfighting, though far more dangerous. It involved a witch or wizard on a broomstick—or any magical creature, really— using whatever means necessary to survive or defeat a dragon. They were given less than four hours to either tame or triumph over the beast.

Another event was a tournament known as Ogre and Troll Wrestling, where competitors battled to prove who was the strongest creature in the realm. The king, however, considered the whole thing foolish. He never believed strength alone was worth proving.

King Jason knew true strength doesn't just come from someone's muscles, but from their heart and mind. As long as someone believes in that kind of strength, nothing else matters.

All the same, Natalia thought those events were the best she'd ever seen. In fact, she loved every one of them.

Nevertheless, after a short break between festivities, she assumed there wouldn't be any more events—and she couldn't have been more wrong.

Soon, she was invited to another spectacle called *broomstick racing*, which was like NASCAR, except it took place in the sky. The races involved countless daring twists, dangerous obstacles, and long, winding laps that were almost impossible to describe. She loved every second of it—and hoped there would be more to come.

Two days later, she got her wish when another event began: *spell fighting*. It was much like a martial arts tournament, except that witches and wizards battled using spells and wands instead of weapons or hand-to-hand combat. However, there were strict rules for this event—no magic that could kill or permanently injure an opponent was ever allowed.

As time went on, the one event Natalia was most looking forward to was the *unicorn races*. It was similar to a horse race—except the riders were witches, wizards, vampires, hags, and more, all mounted on unicorns. The racers and their unicorns were astonishingly fast, far quicker than any horse, making it nearly impossible to catch a clear glimpse of them as they sped by.

Before the race even began—which, by all accounts, was shaping up to be the best one yet—many spectators speculated about who might win, especially since there were several new competitors this year.

Even the king and Natalia found themselves caught up in the excitement, wondering who would claim victory. Though this was Natalia's first time attending the event, she couldn't help but join in the fun and energy of the crowd.

The section of the stands where they sat was the royal box—much like those seen at grand human events. It was crafted from deep red rubies, with a commentary platform directly in front of the king, since it was his duty to start the race.

Natalia sat beside him, dressed in bright blue robes with silver stripes that shimmered in the sunlight.

She looked radiant, but when she noticed the king seemed a bit troubled, she leaned closer and asked softly, "Are you okay, Sire?"

"Not really," he admitted, his voice tired and strained.

Natalia placed a gentle hand on his shoulder.

"What's wrong?" she asked.

He didn't answer right away, but the warmth of her touch seemed to ease him enough to say, "These events are just starting to wear me out."

Natalia was about to respond when a tall male hobgoblin and a troll approached and bowed.

"Your Majesty, we are ready to begin."

"Very well," Jason said.

With that, he rose from his throne and stepped out onto a small balcony overlooking the arena. The crowd erupted into applause as he lifted a hand for silence.

When the cheering faded, he raised his voice—strong and clear enough to be heard in the next two towns—and declared, "Good afternoon, my people, and welcome to the Three-Thousandth Annual Unicorn Race!"

Thunderous applause and cheers filled the air once again.

When it quieted, the king continued, "Our racers this year are..."

He began to announce the names of the fifteen riders and their fifteen unicorns. Each time a name was called, the racers waved proudly to the roaring crowd.

When the introductions were finished, the king raised a hand to quiet the crowd once more.

His voice rang out strong and clear as he said, "Riders, get ready!"

The competitors took their positions, a few of them exchanging sharp, competitive glares.

"On your mark... get set... go!"

At the king's signal, the race began.

About five minutes in, Natalia turned to him and said, "May I ask you something?"

Jason glanced her way.

"That depends on what it is," he replied.

She hesitated, unsure if it was something he'd want to hear.

But finally, she asked, "I just want to know—why do some of these events stress you out so much?"

The king chuckled softly.

"Because, Natalia, it feels like this is *all* I ever do. And it's not just these events—it's everything that comes with being King. Don't get me wrong, I know it's part of the job, but sometimes—"

"You never get any time to yourself," she finished for him, her hand brushing lightly against his.

He looked at her in surprise.

"How did you know that?"

"Everyone knows," she said with a small laugh. "Besides, I overheard you say it a few days ago when you were alone in the rooftop gardens."

At her words, the king looked up at the large scoreboard as the riders passed by for the second lap, noting who was in the lead.

"Well," he said with a wry smile, "I guess it's true what they say. You can't say anything in private in this realm."

"Oh, don't say that, Your Majesty!" came Siberanna's voice from his other side.

He turned to face her.

"Why shouldn't I? It's true."

When no one responded, he sighed lightly and said, "Don't get me wrong, my friends. I've grown to love my job over the years. Still, this isn't what true leadership should always look like—not when there's a risk the power could go to one's head. And even then, the responsibilities can be rather... overwhelming."

"It's just too much sometimes," Natalia added softly, finishing his thought.

The king chuckled and turned to her with a faint smile.

"Yes—and thank you for understanding."

Both of them smiled at each other and turned their attention back to the race—completely unaware that, for the rest of the event, they were still holding hands.

After several hours, the race came to an end. The winner was a young, blonde teenage witch. When the king invited her to approach the royal box, he presented her with a medium-sized golden medal engraved with a large "M" in the center.

After congratulating her and her unicorn for their excellent performance, the king turned to address the crowd. His voice rang out proudly, echoing through the arena.

"I am proud of all the racers who competed today. And yes, even though there can only be one official winner, there are no true winners or losers here—only those who never give up and always give their best."

The crowd erupted into applause, and rightly so. His words were true, and a lesson worth remembering. In every competition, there is no such thing as winning or losing. As long as beings keep trying and never give up on what they love, they're already a winner.

Those who try to make others feel small or stand in the way of their dreams—they're the real losers. Whether out of jealousy or fear of someone else's success, they fail simply because they refuse to try. King Jason knew that anyone could achieve what they set their heart on as long as they take that first step.

Natalia was deeply moved by what the king had said.

When the applause died down, he turned back to the young witch and said warmly, "Today, I offer my heartfelt congratulations to you, Geneva Rodriguez. I'm sure your family will be proud of what you've accomplished—just as I, and everyone here, are proud of you now."

"Thank you, Your Majesty," the young witch said with a bow. "This is truly a dream come true for me... though I doubt my family will see it that way. They never wanted me to do this."

The young witch's words turned the king's smile into a frown.

Placing a gentle hand on her shoulder, he said in an uneasy voice, "And why is that, my dear child?"

She looked up at him and replied softly, "Because, Your Majesty, my family believes this is a waste of time."

Gasps rippled through the crowd. Everyone was stunned by her words.

The king straightened and said firmly, "Well then, young lady, I'll have someone escort you home. And if your parents truly have a problem with you following your dreams, they can expect a summons to the palace."

"That might not be necessary, Sire," Siberanna interjected.

Natalia stepped closer, turning to her friend.

"And why do you say that, Siberanna?"

Siberanna pointed toward the far end of the stands.

"Because her parents are coming this way."

CHAPTER 6

HOW IT ALL STARTED

As the king and the young witch turned to look in the direction Siberanna was pointing, they saw a wizard approaching—a man with a stern, worried expression. He wore light, silvery robes and a matching pointed hat. Beside him walked a witch with white hair, dark lips, and sharp eyes. Her robes were nearly identical to the wizard's, elegant but severe.

When the pair reached the royal box and stopped before their daughter and her unicorn, the young witch tried to speak. Her mother, however, cut her off in a dark and commanding—yet oddly youthful—voice.

"How *dare* you disobey me, young lady? How dare you go against the future we have prepared for you?"

The girl tried again to reason with her parents, but they refused to listen.

Just as her father opened his mouth to speak, the king's voice thundered across the arena.

"Silence!"

Instantly, the crowd fell quiet. A few who met the king's eyes recoiled, frightened by the fury in his expression.

With visible frustration, he looked directly at the young witch's parents and said, "Alton. Fiona. Come with me—we need to have a talk."

At first, the couple tried to protest, but the king raised his voice—nearly shouting—"That's an order! Now come!"

Before leading them away, he turned to the crowd and called out, "Everyone else, you may all head home. Foragon!"

"Yes, Your Majesty," came a deep, rumbling reply.

The speaker was a male minotaur—his body covered in dark gray fur, with the head and torso of a bull but the arms, legs, and hands of a man. He wore a mix of armor and flowing robes, giving him a look both fearsome and dignified.

The minotaur bowed low before the king, who said, "Please see the young witch home while I have a word with her parents."

"As you wish, Your Majesty."

Once the Minotaur and the young rider had departed, the king—accompanied by Siberanna, Natalia, two burly ogres, and a stout dwarf— stepped down from the royal box. Together, they escorted the witch's parents away from the racetrack and into a nearby wooded area.

Both ogres stood firmly behind the young rider's parents, ensuring they didn't try to run. When the king turned to face them and made certain no one else could hear, he cleared his throat.

As he was about to speak, Alton clasped his hands together as if in prayer and said in a trembling voice, "Your Majesty, please understand, we only wanted—"

"Silence!" Jason roared, his voice echoing through the trees.

He began pacing back and forth, anger burning in his eyes.

After a few tense moments, he stopped and said sharply, "Explain yourselves! Why was your daughter afraid to tell you what she wanted to do with her life? You both know I have a law against that!"

Neither of them spoke. The king's fury deepened.

"I am *so* disgusted with you both," he said, his voice low but seething. "I never thought I'd see the Lord and Lady of Cruseutopia defying my law—and yet, here we are."

"Your Majesty!" Fiona, interjected quickly. "Defying you is the last thing we ever wanted to do."

"And," added Alton, "we understand why you created that law, but—"

"But what?" the king snapped, his expression hardening. "If you truly respected the laws that I— and those who ruled before me—put in place, then why are you standing in the way of your daughter's dream to become a championship unicorn racer? Why would you humiliate her, not just before me and the other racers, but in front of everyone who came to witness this race?"

A heavy silence followed. Finally, Fiona spoke, her voice trembling.

"Your Majesty, you must understand... what our daughter wants to do would ruin our family's reputation, and—"

"You stood in the way of your daughter's hopes and dreams," Natalia said sharply, folding her arms across her chest. "All because you were afraid it would ruin your family's reputation. That's just wrong."

And she was absolutely right. Unfortunately, there are people who stand in the way of someone's dreams simply because they don't believe it's the "right" path, or because it's not what *they* want that person to do. As well-meaning as they try to appear, it's clear that they either don't understand or don't care at all. People who destroy another person's dreams, for whatever reason, should not be listened to. Natalia knew if anyone had tried to stop her from doing what she loved, she would have stood up to them and told them that trying to stop someone from following their dreams was wrong in so many ways.

Even so, Alton turned to Natalia and began, "Since when did you—"

"Do not finish that sentence," the king interrupted sharply.

Fiona quickly said, "But, Sire, isn't this the same human—"

"I wouldn't finish that sentence if I were you," Natalia cut in, her tone firm. "And in case you haven't noticed, I'm no longer the spoiled little brat His Majesty once had to deal with. I'm a different person now—someone who not only lives in this realm but is helping to capture Campbell and his two minions, Gorman and Jeffgon."

"That's true," the king said with a proud smile.

Both Alton and Fiona lowered their heads in shame, prompting the king to add in a stern voice, "You two are involved in this effort as well—but that privilege can be easily taken away."

"Sire, please," Fiona said quickly, as she and Alton dropped to their knees.

Alton added in a trembling voice, "You're right. We never should have done what we did, and—"

"Am I to take it," the king interrupted, his tone commanding, "that the moment you return home, you will congratulate your daughter on her magnificent performance today—and not be angry that she defied *your* wishes to follow her own?"

It took a moment for them to respond, but at last they both said "yes" and promised to respect their daughter's dreams—and even help her prepare for next year's race.

The king smiled.

"Very well," he said.

They bowed deeply, and just as they were about to vanish, he added, "But if I hear anything different—and trust me, I *will* know—you both understand what will happen next."

They assured him he wouldn't hear otherwise, and with that, they disappeared into thin air.

Once they were gone, Natalia said softly, "I'm sorry I wasn't much help."

"On the contrary, Natalia," the king said, turning to face her as he stepped closer. "You were all the help I needed."

Those words filled Natalia with pure joy—so much that, before she could stop herself, she did something no one expected. She ran forward and kissed him on the lips.

To her surprise, he kissed her back—without even realizing he was doing it.

No one around them said a word, but the air itself seemed to brighten.

Everyone watching felt the same warmth and hope—and none more so than Siberanna, who whispered to herself, "There is hope. There is hope that we will not lose this king after all."

Meanwhile, far away in Campbell's lair, he and his two minions were stunned by what they had just witnessed. The moment Jason and Natalia broke apart, Campbell waved his hand over the mirror, making it vanish so he could think.

Fury boiled inside him. He let out a long, guttural scream that echoed through the dark cavern. When he finally calmed himself, he began pacing back and forth.

"Master," Gorman said nervously, "you do know what this means, don't you?"

Campbell turned toward her, his eyes blazing.

"Well," she stammered, "they might—"

"*Shut up!*" he roared, blasting her into the wall with a burst of dark energy.

A heavy silence followed.

Jeffgon hurried to help Gorman back to her feet, and the two of them cautiously backed away from their enraged master.

As they tried to slip out of the room, Campbell's voice thundered after them.

"So, she's in love with the boy! And if I don't act soon, she'll rule beside him—as Queen of All That Is Magic—and they'll reign for all eternity! And I'll never take over!"

Both Jeffgon and Gorman returned to their master's side, though Jeffgon kept backing away a little.

"So... what are you going to do, Master?" he asked.

"What do you think I'm going to do?" Campbell snapped.

When no one answered, he sneered, "Why am I surrounded by idiots? Nevertheless—if there's a time to take that girl, it's now."

"But, Master—" Gorman began, and both she and Jeffgon now understood what he intended.

"That girl spends most of her time with the king, his advisors and guards, living in the palace," Campbell growled.

He turned on his minions as they recoiled.

"Do you think I don't know that? She can't stay with him forever. When she's out in the open and unprotected, that's when we strike—and nothing will stand in my way."

As he spoke, a small wet patch in the ceiling shifted and widened until it found an opening in the sewers. It slipped through, emerged into a park, and transformed into a witch who ran toward a thicket where a group of magical creatures waited.

A few steps away, one of them asked, "Did you get his plan?"

"I did," the witch replied. "I recorded everything."

She cast a spell that replayed the scene for the gathered group.

When it ended, one of them said, "The king needs to know about this—and soon. If Campbell ruins any of this—"

"—then we're all in trouble," another finished grimly.

They opened a portal and returned to the Magical Realm to bring their report to the king.

Back at the palace, night had finally fallen. Jason was resting in his room, reading a particularly good book. As he read, his thoughts kept wandering—he couldn't stop wondering why Natalia had done what she did.

Of course, he had enjoyed the moment, but neither of them had spoken on the trip back to the palace. It was hard for him to understand. In the past, she had hated him. Yes, they had grown closer since she'd discovered who he truly was, but this—this was something else entirely.

Jason's room was one of the largest in the palace—far bigger than Natalia's. His bed alone was large enough to fit in a living room, draped in red and gold sheets, pillows, and blankets.

The walls, ceilings, and carpets were all decorated in rich, varying colors. On the far left side of the room stood a wide balcony with a breathtaking view of the magical village below, and several others stretching into the distance.

Directly across from his bed were a pair of tall double doors that opened into the main hallway. To his right stood a walk-in closet and an adjoining bathroom. But perhaps the most remarkable feature of his room was the towering wall of bookshelves, filled to the brim. A large, ornate desk sat before them—where the king often spent hours working on matters of the realm and other affairs.

When Jason finally finished his book, he placed it on the small stool beside his bed and was just about to extinguish the lights and go to sleep when he heard a knock at the door.

Feeling slightly annoyed, he called out, "Who is it?"

"It's Natalia. Do you mind if I come in?"

He froze. This was the first time she had ever come to his room.

Curious and a little uneasy, he said, "You can come in."

The moment she entered, he asked, "What's wrong?"

She didn't answer right away.

Instead, she walked to the right side of his bed, glancing around the room before saying quietly, "Nothing. I just wanted to talk... if that's alright."

He had a feeling he knew what was on her mind, but he simply said, "Of course. What do you want to talk about?"

Silence fell between them for several seconds until she finally murmured that she was sorry for what she had done earlier.

"Why are you sorry for that?" he asked.

"I... I don't know," she said, turning away.

They both laughed softly, the tension between them easing.

Then Jason said, "You look tired. Would you like to lie down and rest for a while?"

He didn't know why he said it—and immediately felt uneasy, wondering what might happen next. Nevertheless, he felt better when she said yes and made room for her to lie down beside him.

For a few quiet moments, neither of them spoke—until Natalia turned to him and said softly, "I thought you were amazing today."

Jason smiled.

"You mean the way I handled those two members of the Rodriguez clan?"

She looked puzzled, which made him pause before realizing she was still new to this realm.

"Well," he explained, "since there's no such thing as death here, many magical families live together in clans, covens, and the like."

"Why is that?" she asked.

"In all honesty, Natalia, I've never quite understood it myself," he admitted with a chuckle. "And you'd think that after so many years as king, I'd understand everything about the Magical Realm."

They both laughed quietly.

Then Natalia said, "All the same, what you did today for that young witch who won the race—that was the best thing I've seen you do since I came here, and—"

She trailed off, but Jason understood what she meant.

"Well," he said, "if there's one thing I won't stand for, as long as I'm king of this realm, it's anyone standing in the way of another person's dreams. It may happen often in the Human Realm, but I'll never allow it here."

They fell into a comfortable silence after that. A few minutes later, Natalia spoke again, her tone a little uneasy.

"There's something I want to ask you."

When he told her to go ahead, he felt a bit uneasy—until she said, "Well... how did all this start? I mean, how did you become king of this realm?"

That was the last thing he'd expected her to ask. He stared up at the ceiling for a few seconds before replying.

"I have to say, that's a wonderful story—if I do say so myself."

"Can I hear it?" she asked eagerly.

It took him a moment to decide where to begin. Finally, stretching his memory, he said, "Well, it all started on the first day of spring, back when we were both in second grade. I had to spend yet another recess sitting in the corner. I hated second grade so much."

"Hey!" she said in a mock-stern voice. "It wasn't just me giving you trouble that year."

"I know that," he said quickly. "Because that was also the year our regular teacher kept being out, and we had that awful substitute who—"

"She had it in for both of us, if you remember," Natalia interrupted with a giggle.

Jason laughed.

"Exactly. Because of that ratbag, I didn't get to enjoy a single recess for the rest of the year."

"I don't think either of us got to enjoy recess in second grade," Natalia said. "I even took a few sick days after everything that happened."

They both laughed, trading a few choice nicknames for their old substitute teacher.

After laughing at one of Jason's more colorful insults, Natalia added, "Still, she got what she deserved the next year—when the FBI arrested her."

They both laughed again.

"I always knew there was something I hated about that sub," Jason said.

"Hey, I hated her too," Natalia replied. "But she got what she deserved, and I hope she rots in jail forever."

They burst out laughing once more before Jason returned to his story. Natalia listened, wide-eyed, as he went on.

"Anyway, that same spring day—right after lunch, actually—when we were heading outside to the playground, I started hearing this strange voice coming from the woods. It was Moongum's voice, echoing through the trees, saying, *'Come into the woods, my boy. Come into the woods.'*"

"And you actually obeyed him?" Natalia said, laughing.

"Hey," Jason said, laughing too, "it was either that or spend another recess getting snarled at by every teacher on duty."

"Just so you know," she said with a chuckle, "a lot of people started looking for you when you disappeared."

"Well, like I said," Jason began, sounding a bit stern. "It was either spend another recess sitting in a corner—which I'd had more than enough of—or follow the voice and see what happened. As I got older, I realized that following an unknown voice is *never* something you should do—because it might just be the last thing you ever do."

Natalia asked, "So, what happened after that?"

It took him a moment to respond as he tried to piece the memory together, but eventually he said,

"Well, after I made sure no one was watching me—especially you, no offense."

"None taken," she said with a grin. "Please, go on."

"Well," he continued, his memories coming back, "as I followed Moongum's voice through the woods, that's when I met Siberanna."

"Siberanna?" Natalia repeated, surprised.

"Yes," Jason said, remembering it all clearly. "She had disguised herself as a four-year-old girl, hanging from a tree and crying. I went over and asked if she was okay, and she said in this tiny, teary voice, *'I'm not. I lost my mommy, and I don't know where she is.'*"

"And when I asked who did this," Jason continued, "she said some big kids had done it because they thought it was funny."

"Then what happened?" Natalia asked.

"Well," he said, his tone softening, "since I was good at climbing back then, I helped her out of the tree and told her we should head back to the school. But she just whined and said, *'I don't want to go near that place. I want to go home.'*"

"So, I asked where she lived and, turns out, it was on the other side of the woods. And yes, I knew that was out of bounds, but I figured, *why not?* I was already stuck spending every recess outside until the end of the year. What else could they do to me—suspend me? At that point, I didn't care if they did."

"Something no one really cares about," Natalia teased. "Suspension just means time off."

They both laughed since it was true. Many students secretly loved being suspended—something no teacher ever seemed to realize.

Jason continued, "A few minutes later, after walking deeper into the woods, we came to a railroad track. As we were almost across, Siberanna got her foot caught on one of the rails."

"She got stuck on the tracks?" Natalia said, shocked.

Jason chuckled.

"Yes—and just as I thought about running back for help, I saw a train speeding straight toward us. So, I did the only thing I could—I tried my hardest to free her."

"You were willing to help someone even when a fast train was about to hit and kill you both?"

He nodded.

"I learned a long time ago that if you ever see someone in trouble and think there's no hope in saving them—you're wrong. There is *always* hope. And if you risk your own life for another, you're a true hero."

After Natalia praised him for his courage, Jason said, "Thanks for that. But after I got her out, we watched the train pass by and then kept walking. As we did, I could hear Moongum's voice again. But then I realized something strange—I didn't know where we were anymore. When I looked back, the tracks were gone, and it felt like we were miles from the school. What I didn't know then was that the moment we crossed those tracks, we had entered the Magical Realm."

"You were already here?" Natalia said, stunned.

Jason chuckled.

"Oh yes. And as I was wondering where we were—because it definitely looked like we were lost—that's when Moongum appeared. He was disguised as an ugly, smelly, frightening hobo, and he jumped out from behind a tree with a knife in his hand."

Natalia gasped, unable to imagine Moongum doing something like that.

Jason nodded.

"I was terrified. But even though I was scared, I told Siberanna to hide behind me while I stood my ground, ready to fight—or at least, I thought I was. Then he said, in this cruel, raspy voice, *You're not afraid of me, boy?* And I told him I was—but I wasn't going to run, hide, or let my new friend get hurt."

"*You have a lot of spirit, boy,*" Moongum said darkly. "*But let's see how brave you are when I stab you in the heart.*"

He came toward me, and though I was terrified, I didn't show it. Just when I thought I was about to die, the knife vanished—and Moongum's real voice returned as he said, "*You have passed the test, Your Majesty.*"

Natalia was stunned.

When she asked what that meant, Jason smiled and said, his voice filled with a mix of pride and awe, "It turned out that helping Siberanna out of that tree, risking my life to save her from the train, and facing Moongum in his disguise were all part of three magical challenges. And by completing them, I earned the right to become king of the Magical Realm—and of All That Is Magic."

Natalia now understood perfectly. And knowing there was still more to come, she stayed quiet as Jason continued.

"I was shocked to hear those words coming from a hobo. Just as I was about to say something, both he and Siberanna transformed back into their true forms—which nearly made me faint.

Siberanna introduced herself first, bowing gracefully and saying, *'I am your first advisor, Sire.'* I couldn't speak after that. Seeing the little girl I'd just rescued turn into a witch who looked like a teenager was almost too much to handle. Still, as she stepped closer, she said, *'Please forgive us for deceiving you, Your Majesty, but it was the only way to ensure you would pass the three challenges of your destiny.'*

Jason paused for a moment, hoping Natalia might say something—but when she didn't, he went on.

"When I finally found my voice, Moongum came up to me and said, in a kind, fatherly tone, *'Please forgive me for scaring you like that. But at least no one saw you when I led you into the woods.'*"

"So, what happened after that?" Natalia asked.

Jason smiled and said, "Well, once I could finally speak, I told them I couldn't do it—being king, I mean. They had already begun explaining what my duties would be, and it all sounded impossible. But they just smiled at each other, and then Siberanna said, *'You're not the first to say those words. Many before you thought they couldn't do this either—but they proved to be the best kings we ever had. And we believe you will be, too, Your Majesty.'"*

He paused for a moment before saying, "I still wasn't keen on taking the job—but then Moongum said something that changed my mind."

"What did he say?"

"He told me it was my choice. I could accept the offer and do something meaningful—something that would help countless people and let me see wonders few humans had ever seen—or I could go back to the life I'd wanted so badly to escape."

"So that's how it all happened?" Natalia asked.

Jason smiled.

"Not quite. After I accepted the offer, I was suddenly teleported here. I spent the next three weeks being taught and trained in everything I needed to know about the Magical Realm—its rules, customs, and history—until the day of my coronation, which I still consider the best day of my life."

"I bet it was!"

"Thanks for saying that," he replied with a grin. "Anyway, on that day, when I first sat on the throne wearing royal robes, with trumpets, drums, and harps playing, I felt both nervous and happy. Then Moongum raised my crown and said, in a deep, commanding voice, *'Jason Wolf, do you swear, as you accept your destiny as our new king, to honor your people and guide them with wisdom, kindness, and courage? Do you promise to protect this realm and its people from any darkness that may arise during your reign? And as you are granted the power to create new laws, do you swear also to honor the ancient laws from the beginning days?"*

"And at the end of that," Jason continued, "I told Moongum and everyone present at my coronation that I swore to do all that—and more. I vowed to be a great king, like those who came before me. The moment I said those words, Moongum placed the crown on my head and proclaimed to everyone, *'Then I now crown thee King Jason Wolf of the Magical Realm.'*

"The second that crown touched my head, I felt an incredible surge of magic fill me. And even though I was only ten, I felt as if I had aged years in that very moment."

"Wow," Natalia said in amazement.

Jason smiled.

"Yes. I spent the rest of that school year here, and during that time, Siberanna used a bit of magic to make sure I wouldn't fall behind. That way, when I returned to the Human Realm, I could still move on to the next grade."

"Well, that explains so much," Natalia said with a grin. "And why you always acted differently whenever I tried to get a reaction out of you."

Jason laughed.

"Well, about a week and a half after becoming king, I met Campbell and his minions—and that's when I learned what true evil looks like."

Natalia laughed softly.

"That's understandable."

"Too bad my time as king is almost over," he said quietly.

She knew those words were coming.

She didn't like them, but she still said, hoping to encourage him, "And who says your time as king has to end?"

He sighed and explained, "Because I can't continue without a queen by my side."

She placed a hand on his chest and said softly, "Jason, please understand... these days I've spent with you have been the best I could ever imagine, and I'm starting to—"

"Natalia," he interrupted gently, taking her arm. "I know what you're trying to say, but please forgive me when I tell you that one of the reasons I took this job in the first place was—"

"Was to get away from me," she finished, her eyes filling with tears.

He winced at the sight of them.

"Not just from you," he said quietly, "but from everything that hurt me. There was nothing left for me in the Human Realm... and you always—"

She cut in again, her voice trembling.

"And how much I wish I could go back in time and stop every bad thing I ever did to you. To take back every cruel word, every awful moment. If I'd known then what I know now, I would have treated you better—been a real friend instead of the school's mean girl."

Her hand moved to his cheek, her voice breaking as she whispered, "Because I love you, Jason. And it's not because you're a king. It's because you're a wonderful, intelligent man who deserves everything he's ever wanted."

Jason felt a deep ache in his chest, and even worse when she began to move off the bed.

"Natalia," he said softly, "you saying these words makes me realize that maybe I've been wrong. But do you—"

"I do mean it!" she cried before he could finish, her voice trembling. "I love you, Jason, with all my heart."

"You do understand," he said, feeling both moved and uncertain, "that if this happens... you'll live forever?"

"So what?" she said, her voice breaking. "I never wanted to die anyway. But does this mean you understand that the person I was—the cruel, shallow girl from the past—is gone? That she's been replaced by someone who loves you?"

He didn't answer. Instead, he pulled her close and kissed her deeply. She kissed him back, and what followed was a very special moment for them both.

CHAPTER 7

THE DATE

News that King Jason and Natalia were finally together spread quickly throughout the Magical Realm. Everyone was thrilled for them—so much so that people wouldn't stop asking when the wedding would be. The constant questions soon began to annoy them both.

After several days of this, Jason and Natalia decided to take some time away from everyone and simply enjoy each other's company.

One afternoon, as they lay on the soft grass in the palace gardens, Natalia sighed and said, "You'd think people would give us time to think about it instead of rushing us."

"I know," Jason said with a small laugh. "But you understand why they're doing this."

Natalia chuckled.

"Yeah, I know, but the year isn't over yet."

"And everyone in this realm knows it," he replied before she could continue. "Still, I don't like being rushed into things. I like to plan ahead—especially since Campbell and his minions are still out there."

"And you don't want to take the risk," she said before he could finish. "You're worried he might try something to ruin this—and honestly, I'm worried about that too."

A moment of silence passed before Jason said quietly, "Looking at what happened to so many before me, I can't help but worry that—"

"Oh, stop worrying about that lunatic," Natalia interrupted gently. "From what the captain told you the other day, they're hot on his trail. It won't be long before he and his minions are gone for good."

They both sat up and looked at each other.

Jason smiled and said, "You always know the right thing to say, Natalia. It's one of the reasons why you're—"

"Oh, stop," she said, laughing.

A few seconds later, they leaned in and began to kiss—softly at first, then with growing warmth as they rolled playfully over the grass.

The garden around them was breathtaking, filled with vibrant flowers of every color and kind, soft emerald-green grass that shimmered under the sunlight, and tall, elegant trees that swayed gently in the breeze. Though not large, the garden was perfectly square, with an enchanted ceiling that mirrored the most beautiful summer sky—a perfect place for them to be alone.

But what Jason and Natalia didn't know was that they were being watched from a distance. The ones watching them were Moongum, Siberanna, and Samantha—who was now a fully formed werewolf—as well as Amanda, who had become a fully formed vampire.

The three, along with Moongum, had been quietly observing the king and the future queen from afar, and all of them thought it was a wonderful sight to see.

However, once they saw Jason and Natalia kissing, they decided to leave—to give them some space and privacy.

As the group walked down another corridor of the palace, Amanda turned to Samantha and said, "Who ever thought this would be possible?"

Samantha laughed.

"Yeah, those two hated each other for most of their lives, and now—"

"And now," Amanda interrupted playfully, "not only are they together, but our best friend is about to become the new queen of this realm."

"And of All That Is Magic as well," Siberanna added with a smile. "I just wish we could get it over and done with already."

Both Amanda and Samantha turned Siberanna to face them, ready to speak—but before either could say a word, Moongum's serious voice cut through the air.

"Siberanna, you of all people know that things like this can't be rushed, as the king himself has said."

"He's right, you know," Amanda added.

"Do you really think I don't know that?" Siberanna said as they began climbing a spiral stone staircase. When they reached the middle landing, she sighed and said, "But the year is almost over, and—"

"It's not coming as fast as you think," Moongum interrupted.

No one spoke after that, and they climbed the rest of the stairs in silence. When they reached the top level of the palace, Moongum finally said, "We've all seen that something real is growing between them. But in case any of you weren't paying attention like I was, they're not rushing things for a reason—they're worried Campbell might be planning something. He's probably found out by now."

Everyone stopped walking and turned toward him.

"What makes you think he'll try something?" Amanda asked.

"Amanda's right," Samantha added. "Everyone's looking for him and his minions. He hasn't been seen since the night we first arrived here."

The group exchanged uneasy looks, and Siberanna said, "That doesn't mean he won't take a risk—especially if it could stop our king from continuing his reign."

"And with the king out of the way—" another creature began.

Amanda and Samantha interrupted together, "We know. Our masters told us."

"Then you two understand just how dangerous and terrible that wizard truly is," Moongum said grimly.

Silence fell again until Samantha asked softly, "What made him like this in the first place?"

"Yeah," Amanda added. "How did it all start? How did he become the greatest threat the Magical Realm has ever faced?"

No one spoke for several seconds.

Finally, in a low, uneasy voice, Moongum said, "No one ever told you the story."

Amanda and Samantha exchanged uneasy looks before Amanda said, "We never really thought about it—until now."

Moongum smiled faintly.

"Then it's time you heard the story," he said. "But not here."

He led them down another hallway, their footsteps echoing softly as they walked for nearly five minutes before arriving at an old, empty room. Once they were certain no one was around, Moongum and Siberanna conjured a set of chairs. When everyone was seated, Moongum began.

"The first thing I need to say," he said, folding his hands, "is that you both know why this realm exists in the first place."

They nodded.

Samantha spoke first.

"Because a long time ago, we tried to live in peace with humans."

"But they feared us," Amanda added. "They were jealous because we could do things they couldn't—along with a bunch of other reasons I'd rather not mention."

Everyone laughed lightly, and then Amanda, still smiling, asked, "But why bring that up now?"

Moongum chuckled and replied, "Because this story begins in the earliest days of the Magical Realm—right after the dark times we had with humans came to an end."

Silence fell over the room as he continued.

"In the beginning, when this realm was first created, it was thanks to a human girl who helped us escape. That's why no human ever saw the great vanishing of the magical creatures. When we finally settled here, the signs and messages from All That Is Magic told us we needed someone to rule over this new realm."

"Wait," Amanda and Samantha said together. "Magic can send messages?"

Moongum nodded and continued, "Indeed. And the messages said that all realms—including ours—were meant to exist for all time. But the ruler chosen to lead us would have to be a being without magic—a creature of the human race. The very kind who banished us... but one who was pure of heart and did not believe in what their kind stood for."

"That's actually a pretty good idea," Samantha said thoughtfully.

"It was," Moongum agreed. "And because of those messages, a brilliant light shone down upon the human girl who had helped us escape the Human Realm. That girl was Queen Morgan. At first, she doubted herself—as did many who would come after her—but the magic entered her mind and showed her the great things she could accomplish. Aside from the king we have now, she became the greatest ruler of her time."

"For in her time, everyone was happy to have her as queen. And for at least five hundred and fifty years, life in this realm was peaceful and prosperous. But—"

"Why did it last only that long?" Amanda and Samantha asked.

Before they could say more, Moongum raised a hand for silence.

"Because there was one person who wasn't happy about it—someone who despised the idea of a human ruling the Magical Realm."

Amanda and Samantha exchanged a knowing glance.

"I'm guessing this person was Campbell," Samantha said.

Everyone in the room laughed.

"Oh yes," Moongum said with a wry smile. "And at first, everyone, even the queen herself, understood where he was coming from."

That confused Amanda and Samantha, so Moongum explained, "Just like you two, he was born into a human family. And back in those days—

before this realm even existed—anyone born with magic to human parents was cast into fire pits."

The girls gasped.

"Humans used to do things like that?"

Moongum nodded and said, "Oh yes. You'd think humans would have improved their behavior over the years—but what they do now isn't much different from what they did back then. The only difference is that now, they do it to each other."

A heavy silence followed. Then Siberanna spoke, her voice uneasy.

"You two still don't understand what it was like for people like us in the Human Realm. And how I wish I could explain it fully. All I can say is that what magical beings endured during the medieval era was far worse than what many people suffer today. It proves that humans have always been violent, cruel, and self-destructive creatures. I still hope one day there might be a way to change that—to help them understand—but perhaps only the next generation can accomplish what so many before them refused to do."

After describing the horrors of the past Moongum continued the story.

"As I was saying, everyone tried to reason with Campbell. Even Queen Morgan herself tried to show him that she wasn't like the humans who had harmed him. But he rejected them all. And what he said to the queen revealed his true nature. He called her a filthy, disgusting animal—someone unworthy of ruling us all."

Moongum paused, his voice growing heavy.

"We were all shocked that he would speak to the queen that way. Even though she herself wasn't offended, the entire Magical Realm was."

"Queen Morgan had long, dark hair, with lips and nails painted a deep red. In her time, she wore the same royal robes that King Jason wears to this day. And when she spoke, it was in a soft Tennessee accent that made every word she said sound graceful and commanding."

After Moongum told Amanda and Samantha how disgusted everyone had been by Campbell's behavior, Samantha asked, "Did she do anything about it?"

"Oh, yes!" Moongum replied emphatically. "That same day, in the throne room, when everyone tried to reason with Campbell, Queen Morgan rose from her throne and said firmly, "Campbell, I don't wish to do this to you, but you've left me no choice. I hereby strip you of your magic and banish you to the Human Realm."

"Before she could complete the spell, his two minions—Gorman and Jeffgon—appeared out of nowhere and blasted the queen with their wands. Fortunately, their attack didn't kill anyone, but it gave them the chance to escape. And from that moment on, the queen knew Campbell had become a grave threat to the entire Magical Realm. Everyone has been searching for him ever since."

"Wow," Samantha whispered, wide-eyed.

Amanda then asked when Campbell had recruited Gorman and Jeffgon. Moongum took a deep breath before answering, clearly uneasy, since it wasn't a topic he liked to discuss.

"Well," he said quietly, "I see we've never quite made it to the middle part of this story."

"But we still haven't gotten to the end," Siberanna said, her voice growing tense.

Moongum sighed.

"The ending," he said gravely, "is the part I'd hoped we'd never have to reach."

"But they're helping us now, Moongum," Siberanna insisted, her tone edging toward panic. "If they're going to face him, they deserve to know just how dangerous Campbell really is."

Another creature spoke up.

"And isn't it only fair that they hear the whole story—especially since the future queen already knows how Campbell became the greatest threat to our realm?"

"Natalia knows?" Amanda and Samantha exclaimed, their voices filled with surprise.

Moongum gave a small chuckle.

"Of course she does. The king told her on the second day after they finally admitted their true feelings for each other."

After a moment of silence, Moongum continued.

"A hundred years before the first ruler of the Magical Realm was forced to see Campbell for what he truly was, he began trying to persuade others that having a human as their queen had been a terrible mistake. Yet no matter how hard he tried, no one agreed. Just as they would with every ruler after her, the people believed Queen Morgan was nothing like the humans who had once persecuted them—or the humans of today. So Campbell found himself alone—except for Gorman and Jeffgon.”

“But why did they join him in the first place?” one of the girls asked.

That question made Siberanna sigh deeply before she began to explain.

“Because they believed he might be right,” Siberanna explained. “They thought that being ruled by someone descended from the very creatures who had banished us in the first place was a mistake.”

Her words made everyone in the room uneasy, but it was something that needed to be said.

“Over the years, many tried to find Campbell, Gorman, and Jeffgon, but no one succeeded. On the rare occasions they emerged from the shadows, they caused terrible destruction in the magical towns and villages that remained loyal to Her Majesty.”

“What happened next, however, was the darkest event in the entire history of the Magical Realm. Before that tragedy, though, the first ruler began receiving signs from magic itself—warnings that it was time for her to find someone to rule beside her. In other words, it was time for her to marry.”

“Wait,” Amanda said, “doesn’t the king only get eleven years to find someone to rule beside him? Why did she get more time than anyone else?”

Moongum laughed softly before answering, “Because magic sensed that she was lonely during her years as queen. Around that same time, humans entered a brief period of peace. They were a little less violent and cruel than before. Sadly, peace among humans never lasts long, since they seem to take pleasure in hurting one another."

He paused, then went on more gently, "But Queen Morgan was cautious about who she dated and who she allowed herself to love. Even during that calmer time, humans still feared what they didn't understand."

"However, she *did* find someone. Her name was Mathilda Brown, and when the queen brought her to the Magical Realm, Mathilda thought it was the most wonderful place she had ever seen. She had every reason to love it, too. Before meeting the first Queen of the Magical Realm, Mathilda's life had been much like the life our king leads today— lonely, difficult, and full of misunderstanding. That was why so many believed she was the perfect person to rule beside the queen."

When Moongum reached this part of the story, he noticed the expressions on Amanda and Samantha's faces.

"Why do you two look so miserable?" he asked.

Amanda sighed.

"From what everyone's told us—and after hearing this story—it feels like the only humans this realm ever trusts are the ones who've been bullied, mistreated, or who never fit in with the rest of humanity."

"Which makes us feel like we really—" Samantha began, her voice trembling.

"Oh, don't say that!" Siberanna interrupted quickly, already knowing what they were thinking. "The reason we trust those kinds of humans is because they understand what it feels like to be unwanted. Humans cast us out for being different—and they cast *them* out for the same reason."

There was a long pause, until Siberanna continued softly.

"But you're both forgetting something important. You—and the queen-to-be—have changed so much since then. You don't need to worry about who you once were. What matters is who you are now."

This made Amanda and Samantha smile, but they still wanted to know what Campbell had done.

"First," Moongum continued, "let me describe who Mathilda was. She had long, light-colored hair, small green eyes, and she dressed in the kind of clothing you might see in the Middle Ages. She spoke with an old-fashioned English accent, gentle yet commanding. When she met the first Queen of the Magical Realm, the two fell deeply in love— each as devoted to the other as the heart could possibly allow."

"But when they decided to marry, everything began to fall apart. On the day of their royal wedding, all was perfect—until Campbell and his minions appeared and destroyed everything. Chaos swept through the celebration. And when Campbell saw that both the queen and her bride-to-be were unprotected, he cast a dark, deadly spell that struck them both down where they stood."

When Moongum reached this part of the story, his voice faltered. He looked uneasy, his expression clouded with grief.

Amanda and Samantha sat in stunned silence, feeling their hearts twist at what they'd just heard.

Everyone in the room felt the same way. None of them had wanted to reach this part of the story.

"All the same," he continued, "after Campbell murdered them, he and his minions vanished without a trace. When others rushed to the fallen queens, ready to help in any way they could, both bodies shimmered—and then dissolved into golden dust, carried away forever."

Everyone fell silent. The weight of his words hung in the air until Amanda finally spoke.

"That's the most horrible thing I've ever heard," she whispered.

Tears filled both her and Samantha's eyes, and even Siberanna's voice trembled as she said, "You're not the only ones who feel that way. On that same day, everyone believed that with the queen's death, all magic would die with her. But the *Chronicle* told us there was another way—that hope was not lost. It was that revelation that began the line of kings and queens who have ruled ever since."

"And the only one who even comes close to being like her," Moongum added, "is the king we have today."

Amanda and Samantha exchanged uneasy glances.

Then Samantha said softly, "So that's why you want him to stay on for all time."

Siberanna gave her a stern look and replied, "It's not just that. He's the last known good human from the Human Realm—and if he steps down, there will be no one left to take his place."

"And," Moongum added firmly, "he's done more for this realm than any ruler before him."

~~~~~

Back in the garden, Jason and Natalia were still enjoying their time together. After their long, tender kiss, they began to talk—about life, about the future, about what might come next. Then, hand in hand, they left the garden and walked down a long marble hallway.

As they strolled beneath the soft glow of the enchanted chandeliers, Natalia looked up at Jason and said, "You know what I can't stop thinking about?"

Jason didn't answer at first. He simply let Natalia continue.

"Why Campbell chose the path he did," she said softly.

A quiet moment passed before they turned a corner, and Jason finally replied, "Well, like I told you, many tried to help him—even the kings and queens before me—but he turned them all away. He believed only in his own ways."
~~~~~

"Just like so many humans," Natalia said, "who still spread fear and hate to this day."

Jason nodded.

"I once told him that very thing. I even said, 'If you hate humans so much, why do you act like them?'"

They both laughed at that, and after a moment Natalia asked, "Did you ever try to help him yourself?"

"I wanted to," Jason admitted. "But everyone warned me it would be a waste of time. After learning what he did to the first queen of this realm, I swore that as long as I was king, I'd do everything in my power to stop him."

Natalia understood why he said that. As they walked further, they came to a cozy sitting area filled with soft armchairs and couches. A grand fireplace glowed warmly at the far end of the room, its light flickering across the polished stone walls. They decided to rest there for a while.

As they sat together on a couch near the fire, Natalia said quietly, "I still can't believe that monster killed the first queen—on her *wedding day,* of all days."

"She wasn't the only one," Jason said darkly, his voice full of disgust.

"Who else?" Natalia asked.

And that's when he began to tell her about the seven others Campbell had murdered.

Jason's voice grew quiet as he went on to say, "Even though I understand what he went through before the Magical Realm existed—"

"But what *he* needs to understand," Natalia interrupted, placing a gentle hand on his shoulder, "is that we didn't choose to be his enemies. He did this to himself. That's why he's not just a threat to the Magical Realm—but to himself as well."

Jason nodded in agreement. She was right, and he knew it. Her words earned her another soft kiss, and the two of them spent the rest of the day together. With no royal duties to attend to, Jason was simply happy to enjoy the company of the woman he had once despised—but now loved more than he could ever admit.

A few days later, back at Northburg School, Jason sat alone during lunch, half asleep over a barely touched sandwich.

Natalia appeared beside him and said, smiling, "You alright?"

"I'm fine," he said with a long yawn. "Just tired. I'm *always* tired when I have to be in the Human Realm."

They both laughed, and several students turned to stare at them in disbelief. Natalia noticed and gave a playful nod to a few of them before turning back to Jason.

"You'd think people would have something better to stare at," she said with a grin.

Jason chuckled.

"Well, Natalia, we did spend most of our lives hating each other—"

"And now," she cut in with a teasing smile, "we're boyfriend and girlfriend—and soon to be more than that."

Jason quickly stopped her from finishing that sentence. It wasn't something they could talk about openly in the Human Realm.

Still, when they heard a few people whispering nearby, Natalia sighed and said, clearly annoyed, "I know everyone's surprised, but you'd think they'd find something else to talk about."

Ever since the new school year began, and since both she and Jason still had to keep up their lives in the Human Realm, everyone had been stunned to see them together—holding hands, laughing, and even sitting next to each other.

A few of the teachers had been just as surprised, one of them even muttering, "Am I seeing what I *think* I'm seeing?"

The two of them did their best to ignore the attention.

Then Natalia leaned closer and said with a playful smile, "Hey, since you don't have any royal meetings or magical duties this afternoon, how about a movie at the Northburg Theater?"

He wanted to say yes, but the words wouldn't come out.

Sensing this, Natalia placed her hand over his and whispered so only he could hear, "I know you're worried about Campbell since he's somewhere in this area—but that doesn't mean we shouldn't take a little risk."

Her words made him smile.

Just as he was about to respond, she added softly, "Besides, you've got some pretty great protectors. If Campbell tries anything, we'll be ready."

She wasn't wrong. Surrounding their table—visible only to them—stood a discreet ring of guards: several powerful witches and wizards, two stern-looking centaurs, an ogre, and a troll.

When Jason opened his mouth to say something, the troll leaned in and rumbled, "She's right, Sire. We can't take him head-on if he strikes right now, but you and the lady deserve a night out."

Jason tried again to speak, but then a witch whispered, "Your Majesty, the two of you *need* a little time away from the Magical Realm."

"And again, Your Majesty," one of the centaurs added firmly, "if he dares come for you, we'll be ready."

"And if anything does come up," Natalia said, knowing he was already thinking about it, "I asked Siberanna to put everything on hold. So you'll have no excuse not to go."

"You did that for me?" he asked, smiling.

She smiled back.

"Of course I did."

"Well then," he said, relaxing a little, "what movie do you want to see?"

As they began deciding, neither of them realized that Gorman and Jeffgon were watching from above through the sky windows.

Once they'd heard enough, the two slipped away.

~~~~

Up on the school roof, Gorman stopped and said, "Do you think we should take this information back to Campbell—or try something ourselves?"

Jeffgon laughed dryly, and replied, "You really think we can pull something off on our own?"

Gorman thought for a moment, then said, "Good point. But since we've failed him so many times, maybe this could earn us some respect."

"You know that's easier said than done," Jeffgon replied warily.

Gorman shot him a sharp look, and the two fell silent for a moment before she muttered, "I guess you're right. Let's just head back and see if Campbell already has a plan."

"And knowing him," Jeffgon said in a low, uneasy voice, "he always does."

With that, both of them vanished into a swirl of dark dust.

~~~~~

Later that day, after school, Jason and Natalia arrived at the Northburg Movie Theater to decide which film to see. It had one of the largest lobbies ever built. Its ceiling was lined with skylights, and on each side of the grand entrance stood a small ticket counter. The theater also boasted a huge arcade filled with every kind of game imaginable and two long hallways leading to the auditoriums.

But the best part of all was the snack bar—a massive counter overflowing with every treat you could think of.

When it was their turn at the ticket desk, the attendant smiled and asked, "Which movie would you like to see?"

After they made their choice, two tickets slid out from a narrow slot.

Jason handed over the money, and as the attendant passed them their tickets, she said, "Your movie starts in fifteen minutes in Theatre Four. Just head down the hallway on the left—and enjoy the show!"

"We will!" Jason and Natalia said together.

They walked over to the snack bar next, and when their turn came, Jason began ordering food like he hadn't eaten all day.

"Okay, that's enough," Natalia said firmly.

"But I haven't even gotten to the candy yet," Jason protested.

She gave him a mock glare.

"You shouldn't be eating so much junk food anyway."

He hadn't expected her to say that, so he quickly replied, "That's not true."

Natalia gave him a skeptical look, prompting him to add with a grin, "Junk food's good for you— it's always been good for my people."

Before she could respond, the snack bar worker interrupted politely.

"Excuse me, but you're holding up the line. If you're done ordering, please let me help the next guest."

"Right, sorry," Jason said quickly.

They grabbed two large drinks and, after a short wait for their food, headed down the left hallway to find their theater.

It didn't take them long. The auditorium they entered was massive—wide rows that climbed toward the projection booth, plush seats, and a huge glowing screen already playing pre-show slides.

After settling into their seats near the middle, they watched the previews in comfortable silence. After a few minutes, Jason noticed Natalia looked distracted.

"What's wrong?" he asked softly.

She sighed and said, "Well... you know this year's almost over."

Those were the last words he'd wanted to hear.

Just as he started to speak, she continued, "And I know things are finally going well for us, and—"

"I know what you're trying to say, Natalia," he cut in gently, "and I do want it to happen—but..."

"But what?" she asked softly.

It took him a moment to respond. The way she'd said it made his heart ache.

When he finally found his voice, he said, "With Campbell still out there—and so close, too—I'm afraid he'll try to do something to us. Just like he did to Queen Morgan and her bride-to-be. And I don't want to rush things because... I'm afraid something will go wrong."

Natalia smiled faintly, her eyes warm.

"That's understandable. I don't want anything to go wrong either, but I'm the one rushing this, not you. Because not only do I want you to stay king forever—I love you. And yes, I know we're too young to get married. But like a wise old wizard once said, 'If you love someone deeply, why wait for the time others think you're ready?'"

He knew exactly which wizard she was talking about—Moongum—and he silently agreed.

He was about to say something, when the theater screen flickered, stretching wider than any screen he'd ever seen. For a few minutes, they watched trailers for upcoming movies, then the lights dimmed, and the feature began.

The film was a romantic comedy with plenty of action, and they enjoyed every moment of it. During one scene, something in the story struck Jason deeply. That was when he finally made a decision— one that caused something small and mysterious to appear in his pocket.

When the three-hour movie ended—it had been long but worth every minute—they stayed through the credits, gathering up their trash.

"I hate doing this part," Natalia said with a sigh.

"I'll do it all if you want," Jason offered with a smile.

She felt bad and quickly said, "I didn't mean it like that."

They both laughed, tossing the last of their trash before leaving the auditorium through an exit that led into the woods behind the theater.

They could have opened a portal back to the Magical Realm, but as they took a few steps into the trees, Jason suddenly stopped.

When Natalia noticed, she turned to him and asked softly, "Are you alright?"

"I'm fine," he began, but when he looked at her, his nerves started to get the better of him. "I was just thinking..."

"About what?" she asked, feeling a little nervous herself.

For a moment, neither of them spoke.

Then Jason finally said, "That scene in the movie—and what you said earlier—made me realize you were right. We *are* ready. And we do love each other... more than anything."

"Does this mean...?" Natalia began, her voice trembling with happiness.

Before she could finish, Jason dropped to one knee and took a golden ring from his pocket.

"Natalia Summers," he said, his voice steady but full of emotion, "would you do me the—"

"Yes!" she exclaimed, her voice bursting with joy.

Before they knew it, they were kissing. When they finally paused, Jason slipped the ring onto her finger, and both of them laughed softly, overwhelmed by the moment.

It felt like the most magical thing either of them had ever experienced. Jason and Natalia knew they truly loved each other, and their hearts knew they wanted to spend their lives together; so why hold back? They were no longer willing to allow delays or let fear keep them from happiness. After all, this might be their only chance, and they didn't want to risk someone else coming along and taking them away from each other.

They realized then that love is its own kind of magic—the greatest kind there is. And as long as they brought out the best in each other their lives would be filled with light. That's all the magic they would ever need, for magic is more than just spells, curses, enchantments, and waving a wand around. It's about finding true happiness in life—and having someone wonderful to share that life with.

When Jason and Natalia's moment ended and they stood again, Jason wrapped an arm around her and said softly, "Come on, let's go home."

"Let's," she replied with a smile.

However, just as they were about to open a portal, a low, cruel laugh echoed through the woods—coming from nowhere and everywhere at once. They both froze, already knowing who it was before Campbell and his two minions materialized before them.

The first thing Campbell said, his voice dripping with malice as he stepped closer, was, "I must admit, I never thought I'd see this day. I never imagined *you* would be the one he'd choose to rule beside him for all eternity."

Jason was about to respond, but Natalia spoke first, her tone sharp with disgust.

"You dare speak of something you have no right to talk about?"

"And you dare," Gorman sneered, her lips curling into a wicked grin, "speak to the most powerful wizard in such a tone?"

"I decide, Gorman," Jason said through gritted teeth, "who the most powerful witch or wizard is. And when I look at Campbell, I don't see power—I see the greatest threat to every realm in existence."

Campbell threw his head back and laughed.

"We'll see about that. It won't be long before *all* the realms are under my control."

Both Jason and Natalia laughed in return.

Jason met his gaze and said firmly, "That will never happen—as long as I'm king."

"Which won't be long for you," Jeffgon added with a wicked chuckle.

But when he saw Jason and Natalia still laughing, his grin faltered.

Jeffgon wanted to ask why they were laughing, but before he could, Natalia said coolly, "If I were you three, I'd stop talking before things get ugly."

"And what makes you say that, my dear?" Campbell sneered.

"First of all, Campbell," Natalia shot back, her anger rising as she raised a clenched fist toward him. "Don't ever talk to me like that again. And second—because I believe you three are about to wish you never came here."

"Oh really?" Campbell said, his eyebrows lifting in surprise.

He and his two minions exchanged uneasy glances—just as Jason and Natalia gave a sharp, echoing whistle.

In an instant, magical energy filled the air. Out of shimmering portals appeared Siberanna, Moongum, Amanda, and Samantha—followed by three trolls, a banshee, two centaurs, an ogre, several hags, and even a towering giant. They all surrounded Campbell and his minions, their eyes glowing with power.

Campbell let out a low growl.

"So, Jason… still setting traps for me, are we?"

"That's right, Campbell," Jason said with biting sarcasm, folding his arms. "And I'm only going to say this once. You and your loyal lapdogs, Gorman and Jeffgon, are to surrender immediately and face judgment for your crimes. You can kneel and make this easy—or we can do it the hard way."

"I will never accept defeat!" Campbell roared, drawing his wand as his minions followed suit. "I will never take orders from *you*, Jason—or from *you*, Natalia—or from any of your pathetic—"

"Silence!" Jason and Natalia commanded in unison.

Then Jason stepped forward and said, "Very well, Campbell," Jason said, his tone cold. "I tried to be fair and reasonable—but as always, we have to do it *your* way."

And with those words, the battle began.

Even though Campbell and his minions were outnumbered, they fought fiercely. Bolts of magic and bursts of fire lit up the clearing as spells clashed in midair. Two witches, along with Samantha and Amanda, stayed close to Jason and Natalia to protect them from the crossfire.

But when Jason saw that his people were struggling, he tried to rush into the fight.

"Your Majesty, please!" one of the witches cried, holding him back. "You'll be walking right into his trap!"

"I don't care!" Jason shouted, trying to break free. "I'm not going to stand by and watch my people—"

Before he could finish, Campbell and his minions unleashed a massive blast that sent everyone crashing to the ground. Then, turning his wand on Jason and Natalia's protectors, Campbell forced them back with a storm of dark energy.

That was the moment Jason and Natalia joined the fight. As they confronted Campbell, Amanda and Samantha turned their fury on Gorman—who quickly realized she was no match for a vampire and a werewolf. At the same time, Jeffgon fought the two witches, but he too was outmatched.

For a brief moment, it seemed the battle could go either way. Then Campbell struck with deadly precision, blasting Jason off his feet and sending shockwaves through the clearing. One by one, Jason's allies fell to the ground.

Standing over Jason's unconscious body, Campbell let out a cruel laugh.

"You've lost, Jason," he said, his voice thick with triumph. "Not only have you failed to stop me, but now I have the one thing that kept you strong.

With her in my hands, the walls that once stood in my way will crumble. After centuries of waiting, I will finally rule *all* the realms—and the world will bend to my will."

He kicked Jason hard in the face, then vanished in a cloud of dark smoke—taking Natalia with him.

CHAPTER 8

SAVING NATALIA

The moment Jason and the others regained consciousness, he was horrified to see that Natalia was gone.

Just as he was about to speak, Moongum appeared beside him and said urgently, "Lie still, Sire. You're injured, and—"

"I don't care!" Jason shouted, struggling to get up, but Moongum pressed him back down.

"All I want to know," Jason growled, his voice trembling with fury, "is what happened to Natalia?"

"I'm afraid Campbell has taken her, Your Majesty," Moongum said quietly, his tone filled with dread.

At those words, Jason froze in stunned silence. His hands clenched, and he was just about to let out a roar of rage when Moongum stopped him.

"Sire, please! If you scream, the humans will find us. But don't worry about Natalia—everything is under control."

Jason shot him a desperate look.

"What do you mean?"

~~~~~

Campbell was back home in his lair, where the dark wizard was already savoring his triumph.

In the dim, flickering light of the underground chamber, Gorman and Jeffgon used their wands to chain Natalia's wrists to the ceiling and her feet to the floor with heavy bands of magic. Campbell stepped forward, a cruel grin twisting his face.

Just as he was about to speak, Natalia spat in his face.

With a voice filled with hatred, she snarled, "You made a big mistake capturing me, Campbell."

"And what makes you say that, my dear?" Campbell sneered, laughing wickedly.

Natalia smirked, fire flashing in her eyes.

"You don't really think Jason's going to stop until he finds me, do you?"

Campbell and his minions laughed at her defiance.

"Even if Jason *does* come for you," Campbell sneered, "he'll never find you. No one ever has—and no one ever will."
~~~~~

Natalia chuckled softly.

"That's because you never stay in one place for too long."

Those were the last words any of them expected to hear. The laughter died instantly. Campbell's face twisted with shock, then fury. In a flash, he seized Natalia by the throat.

"How do you know about that?" he roared, his voice trembling with rage. "No one knows that—not even Jason!"

"He does now," she rasped through her tightening throat. "Because I told him."

At her words, Campbell's expression darkened, and both Gorman and Jeffgon exchanged uneasy glances.

Campbell shook her violently and hissed, "You're going to tell me how you found out I've been moving from place to place—or—"

"Or what?" Natalia cut in, her voice dripping with sarcasm and a defiant smile on her face. "You'll kill me? That won't help you, Campbell. It'll just make things worse for you."

Campbell released her, stepping back, his fury boiling beneath the surface. Her words only made him more frustrated—and that made her laugh even harder.

"You think you're funny, do you?" he growled.

"I *know* I am," she shot back.

Gorman and Jeffgon raised their wands, ready to curse her, but Campbell threw out a hand.

"Stand down," he ordered coldly. "She's only trying to provoke us—just like she used to do to Jason, before she decided he was worth her time."

At those words, Natalia's laughter vanished. Her eyes blazed with anger.

"Don't you *dare* bring that up, Campbell!" she shouted, her voice echoing off the stone walls.

"Why not?" Campbell snapped, laughing as his minions joined in.

Just as Natalia opened her mouth to respond, he said mockingly, "It's something I've always wondered. You and Jason hated each other for most of your lives. Then suddenly, you discover his secret—and now you're in love?"

Before she could answer, Jeffgon stepped forward with a wicked grin.

"You know, Master, I think I know the *real* reason she loves Jason now."

"Oh, please—do tell," Campbell said, smirking as he turned to him.

"Well, Master," Jeffgon began slyly, "human girls like her are usually gold diggers. And since, in the Human realm, being royalty means—"

"That is *not* the reason I love him!" Natalia cut in, her voice rising with fury. "How dare you think I'd ever do something so shallow? I may have been mean and awful in the past, but if there's one thing I would *never* do, it's love someone for their money. No one should ever love someone just because they're wealthy or successful. That's one of the cruelest and emptiest things a person can do."

Natalia went on, her voice shaking but strong.

"I'll always feel guilty for the horrible things I did to him. Yes, he's forgiven me—but I haven't forgiven myself. And maybe I never will."

All three of them burst into cruel laughter.

When they finally stopped, Campbell said with a cold smile, "Well, Natalia, as touching as all of that was—it doesn't matter. Jason will never find you. Which means I've already won... and he's lost."

He and his minions turned to leave, but before they could take more than a few steps, Natalia said, "You know, Campbell, not only does everyone in the Magical Realm hate you—they also *pity* you."

Without turning around, Campbell froze.

"What do you mean?" he demanded.

"I mean," she said softly, "everyone knows the terrible things humans did to you when you were younger—what led you down this path."

"*Shut up!*" Campbell snapped, spinning around and pointing his wand at her. "How dare you bring that up? How dare you talk about something you don't understand?"

"Oh, I understand perfectly," Natalia said, her voice edged with sarcasm. "I know what it's like when your parents don't love you."

Campbell's face twisted—not just with anger, but with something that almost looked like fear.

"Because my parents didn't seem to love me either," she went on, "even though—"

"My parents didn't *try to throw me into a fire pit* because I wasn't human!" Campbell shouted, his voice breaking.

Natalia waited for him to calm down, then said quietly, "I understand that, Campbell. But instead of letting it go, you turned your anger and hate against the very ones who tried to help you."

"Help me?" he roared, his fury rising again. "Is *that* what everyone says they were trying to do? Lies! All they wanted was to force me to live by their precious laws of 'good' magic—a system ruled by the same creatures who destroyed me in the first place!"

Natalia nodded slowly, her expression heavy with disappointment.

When she didn't speak, Campbell sneered. "What's this? Nothing more to say?"

"It's not that, Campbell," she said sadly. "I'm just realizing what every king and queen before Jason saw—that there's no hope left for—"

She didn't finish. Campbell struck her hard across the face.

"I'm *sick* of the way you talk to me!" he bellowed.

"Well, maybe it's about time someone did," Natalia shot back. "Too bad your minions are too scared to stand up to you. But then again, you can't seem to go a single day without blasting them around with your wand."

Once again, Campbell and his minions froze in shock. All three began whispering among themselves, their voices filled with panic.

"How does she know all this?"

They were clearly worried about what else she might know.

Campbell raised his wand and pointed it directly at her throat.

"Well, my dear," he said darkly, "since you know *too much*, I can't allow you to live. So—"

Before he could finish the spell, iron shackles suddenly appeared around his arms, forcing him to drop his wand. In the same instant, he and his minions were yanked backward and slammed against a stone wall, held fast by invisible magic.

Before they could react, King Jason, Siberanna, Moongum, Amanda, Samantha, and several others appeared in Campbell's lair. Campbell and his followers scowled—cornered at last.

Jason rushed to Natalia's side, magically releasing her from the chains.

She threw her arms around him, kissing him again and again before crying, "What took you so long?"

"My fault," Jason said as they pulled apart. "No one told me this was *your* plan—to finally capture Campbell and his minions."

Natalia giggled, her smile bright through her tears.

"I'm sorry I didn't tell you," she said softly. "But I thought if I did, it might ruin the best time I've ever spent with you."

Both of them laughed before Jason said, "I'll admit—that was a brilliant plan. I didn't like that you were putting your life at risk, but once again, you've proven how clever you are."

They were about to kiss again when Campbell shouted, "This was another trap?"

Everyone laughed.

Jason and Natalia walked up to face him, and Natalia said, "Yes, Campbell—it *was* a trap. Knowing you'd do anything to stop Jason from remaining king, I knew I had to act."

She paused, hoping he'd respond, but when he didn't, she went on.

"Everything was part of the setup. Jason and I, out in the open without protection. Losing the fight to you. And the moment you captured me, a tracking spell activated. That's what led everyone here. It's over, Campbell—you and your minions are finished."

Campbell's face twisted with rage.

"You can't talk to us like that—or do this to us!"

Laughter filled the room again.

Jason placed a hand on Natalia's shoulder and said, "Actually, Campbell, she *can*."

Campbell glared at him, ready to speak, but Natalia raised her hand, flashing the golden ring on her finger.

"Just before you kidnapped me, Jason proposed. I'm the queen-to-be now."

"Which means," Siberanna said, pointing her wand at Campbell and his minions, "she has the authority to give commands."

Campbell's fury boiled over.

"If you think I'm going down that easily, then—"

Before he could finish, dark sparks shot from the spot where his wand had fallen. He and his minions suddenly broke free—but when they tried to vanish, nothing happened.

"Don't bother," Jason said, his voice calm and commanding. "A containment spell was cast over this entire place. You won't be going anywhere."

"If you think this will keep me here, you're wrong," Campbell snarled.

Everyone laughed, and Natalia said, "I wouldn't bet on it. The spell that was cast on me didn't just help us find you—it also reacted with your own magic. The spells you used to break free have now corrupted your power. Any future magic you try to use will fail."

Jason stepped forward, his tone firm and steady.

"So now, you have no choice but to surrender. It's over for you, Campbell. You and your followers—"

Campbell suddenly lunged forward, charging at them.

Before he could get close, Siberanna and Moongum raised their wands and blasted him and his minions back against the wall.

Jason turned to Natalia and asked with a small smile, "Would you like to do the honors?"

"I think so," she said, stepping forward confidently.

She raised her wand and declared, "Campbell, Gorman, and Jeffgon—your crimes against the Magical Realm are unforgivable. For these crimes and more, I hereby strip you of your magic and banish you to the Human Realm for the rest of your days."

The moment she finished, Jason clapped his hands. Streaks of light burst from the three captives, swirling into a glowing orb that floated between them. Jason reached out, crushed it in his hand, and as he did, Campbell and his minions screamed. Their bodies lifted into the air and shot upward like streaks of fire—vanishing forever.

When the light faded, Jason turned to his people and said, "We did it, everyone. We finally did it."

The room erupted with cheers and applause.

Moongum stepped forward and bowed.

"No, Your Majesty—you did it. You accomplished what so many before you could not. With Campbell banished and powerless, our troubles are over—for now."

Jason nodded, understanding his meaning.

Natalia said with a bright smile, "And now that Campbell's gone, we don't have to worry about him crashing our wedding."

The moment she said it, everyone began speaking at once.

"When is it?!"

"When's the big day?"

"How soon?"

Jason raised his hands to calm the crowd.

"That," he said with a grin, "is something we don't know yet—because—"

"Your Majesties," Siberanna said, bowing slightly, "I'd like to volunteer to organize everything. If I can gather the right people—and if you write down everything you want and need—I can have your special day ready in less than two weeks."

Natalia and Jason exchanged a warm look, then nodded in agreement.

"Very well," Jason said with a smile. "You have our blessing to handle it."

CHAPTER 9

A WHOLE NEW BEGINNING

The day of the royal magical wedding finally arrived, and the entire Magical Realm buzzed with excitement—but no one was more thrilled than the bride and groom themselves.

The ceremony took place in a vast forest, where soft green grass spread beneath towering trees that encircled the entire area like silent guardians. Flowers of every color and kind bloomed in dazzling abundance, their scent drifting gently through the air.

The dining area gleamed with tables and chairs crafted from silver and gold, all set near the far end beneath a shimmering diamond-colored tent prepared for the celebration to follow.

Thousands upon thousands of golden chairs lined both sides of the long, colorful carpeted aisle—each perfectly sized to accommodate creatures of every shape and height. The entire Magical Realm had gathered for this day, and not a single seat was left empty.

Along the left side of the aisle sat the musicians—fauns and satyrs—gracefully playing harps, flutes, and violins. Their soft melody filled the air as guests found their seats and turned their eyes toward the front.

On the left stood the bridesmaids, Amanda and Samantha, radiant in gowns more beautiful than any ever seen at a royal wedding. Each held a delicate bundle of flowers, their colors shimmering like the dawn.

Everyone at the wedding was dressed in the finest tuxedos and gowns imaginable, but none of the guests wore white—because, as everyone knows, you never wear white to a wedding.

On the groom's side stood a centaur and a minotaur as groomsmen, with an ogre serving as best man. Jason had chosen these three because they had been his closest friends ever since he became king.

Nevertheless, the three stood proudly by Jason, who looked striking in a light-white tuxedo that made him appear every bit the royal groom. As he spoke with his friends, feeling a touch of nervousness, they helped calm him down with reassuring words and laughter.

Just as Jason began to relax, Moongum appeared out of thin air. He was to serve as minister for the ceremony.

Looking around at the gathered crowd, he raised his voice so all could hear.

"Please be seated, everyone."

He then stepped back from the groom, groomsmen, and bridesmaids. His robes shimmered faintly—light, clear wizard's robes paired with a matching pointed hat—and he carried a small book in one hand.

After a brief moment of silence, Moongum gave a subtle signal to the musicians. Instantly, the air filled with gentle music. Forest and water nymphs, serving as flower girls, began to dance gracefully down the aisle, scattering petals of every color as they went.

No sooner had the flower girls finished than the music changed—signaling everyone to turn toward the back.

And there she was—the bride—appearing as if from thin air, radiant and graceful as she began her walk down the aisle. One by one, guests rose and bowed in respect as she passed.

Natalia wore the most breathtaking wedding gown any girl could ever dream of. She looked like the most beautiful woman in all the realms.

Since Natalia's parents weren't allowed in the Magical Realm, she had to make the walk alone. She didn't mind—not one bit. In fact, she carried herself with such quiet pride and confidence that everyone watching felt their hearts swell with admiration. When at last she reached the front, she took Jason's hand, and the crowd erupted into applause.

As silence settled over the gathering, Moongum opened his small book and spoke in a clear, commanding voice that echoed through the forest.

"Citizens of the Magical Realm, we are gathered here today to unite the lives of King Jason Wolf and Natalia Summers as one."

A hush fell over everyone. The moment was so moving that all in attendance could feel a lump forming in their throats.

Turning to Jason, Moongum continued, "Do you, King Jason Wolf, take Natalia Summers to be your loving wife—to have and to hold for all time to come?"

"I do," Jason said, his voice warm and sure, though his cheeks turned a bright shade of red— which brought tears to Natalia's eyes.

Everyone in the crowd gushed, "Aww!"

The sound rippled through the forest for several seconds before fading away.

When it quieted, Moongum turned to Natalia and began, "And do you, Natalia—"

"I do!" she said, cutting him off with cheerful impatience.

Her quick reply brought joyful laughter and happy tears to nearly every face in attendance. Those sitting near a few giants even had to open umbrellas, as the giants' tears fell like raindrops.

Both Jason and Natalia felt an overwhelming mix of happiness and emotion—something that often happens on days as grand as this.

Even Moongum had to steady himself, his voice trembling slightly as he asked, "Who would like to give their vows first?"

It took a moment for them to decide, but at last Jason spoke, his tone soft yet full of feeling.

"Natalia Summers, even though we spent most of our lives fighting and hating each other, I want you to know how grateful I am to be marrying you. It's not because I want to remain king—but because I finally see what I should have seen long ago—that you're the one I want to spend all eternity with."

As he spoke, the crowd sighed and sniffled, their hearts melting at his words. Natalia herself thought it was the most beautiful thing she had ever heard.

When it was her turn, she said,

"Jason Wolf, the vows you gave me were wonderful. And the ones I have for you are simple. Yes, those bad days between us are over, and a great future lies ahead. I promise to be a loyal and honest wife and to help you in every way I can to make the Magical Realm an even more wonderful place to live."

It was a vow both tender and sincere—and everyone agreed it was perfect.

After a brief pause, Moongum smiled and said, "Who has the rings?"

The ring bearer—a small female brownie—stepped forward, holding a tiny pillow trimmed with ruby-red ribbon. Upon it rested two gleaming golden rings.

When she lifted the pillow, the real magic began. Both rings rose into the air on their own, floating gently before sliding perfectly onto the bride and groom's fingers. The instant they did, a soft, shimmering force field surrounded Jason and Natalia in a luminous circle that spun gently around them before fading away into the air.

Although Jason and Natalia were astonished by what had just happened, curiosity quickly replaced their wonder.

"What was that?" they both asked at once.

Moongum chuckled softly.

"That," he said, "was the magical bond—an eternal connection that joins two souls who were truly meant to be together."

The couple gazed at each other in awe, their smiles widening.

After a brief moment, Moongum cleared his throat and said, "Shall we continue?"

Everyone fell silent as he raised his book once more and declared, "By the power vested in me, by the ancient laws of magic, and by King Jason Wolf himself, I now pronounce you husband and wife. You may now kiss the bride."

But Jason and Natalia didn't wait for him to finish. They were already kissing before he reached the second sentence, which made Moongum pause, grin, and chuckle.

Finally, he turned to the crowd and announced with joy, "Citizens of the Magical Realm, I present to you King Jason and Queen Natalia of the Magical Realm!"

Everyone clapped and cheered as Jason and Natalia walked hand in hand toward the tent area for the after-party.

Just before entering the tent, the bride and groom stopped at the entrance. Natalia turned to the crowd to take part in a beloved old wedding tradition. With a playful smile, she tossed her bouquet high into the air—and instantly, a flurry of female magical creatures scrambled to catch it.

The lucky one who did was Geneva, the young witch who had won the last unicorn race. When the flowers landed in her hands, she felt as if she had just won all over again.

The after-party that followed was the grandest celebration the Magical Realm had ever seen. Everyone ate, drank, danced, laughed, and talked long into the night. Joy filled the air like music itself.

One by one, guests stood to make toasts to the newlyweds—offering warm wishes such as, "Congratulations to the happy couple!" and "Long live the King and Queen!"

"Congratulations to King Jason and Queen Natalia, the rulers of the Magical Realm!"

"I always thought the king might never find someone to rule by his side—but how wrong I was. What a wonderful couple the king and queen make! I'm happy to say the golden age of our realm will never end."

"At first, I was shocked that the future queen would be the very girl who once made the king's life a living nightmare in the Human Realm—but now I see they are truly a match made of pure magic."

"Now that the king is married, not only will he continue his reign, but he also has someone by his side for all time to come."

"May you both have a long, happy, and magical life together!"

Many more kind words followed, each toast warmer than the last. After a few minutes, Amanda and Samantha came up to the couple to offer their own congratulations.

After a moment of laughter and smiles, Amanda said, "Who would have thought this a few months ago?"

"What do you mean?" Natalia asked, her voice bright with glee.

Samantha grinned and said, "Well, a few months ago, the two of you fought like cats and dogs—and now you're husband and wife, ruling the Magical Realm together."

They all burst out laughing at the irony.

~~~~~

"It really was the best day your father and I ever had!"

Natalia smiled several years later. She now wore elegant royal robes and a small tiara, seated comfortably in an armchair within a cozy room. She looked older, wiser, and more serene.
~~~~~

Years had passed since her wedding day, and Queen Natalia was now telling the story of that magical day to her children.

"After the party," she said with a fond smile, "your father told me he had a surprise for me."

"What was it, Mom?" asked a little girl with short white hair, dressed in dark blue robes.

Turning toward her, Natalia replied, "Well, Jane, your father said he had a vacation house in one of the most beautiful spots in our realm. He thought it would be the perfect place to spend our honeymoon."

There was a brief silence before a teenage boy with light-colored hair, wearing light brown robes said in a kind but teasing tone, "Isn't that the same place we all go to whenever you and Dad need to get away from it all?"

Natalia laughed.

"That's true, Mason. And as I've said before, no one but us knows about it. Because if everyone knew where we go to rest—"

"Then we'd never be left alone!" all of her children finished in unison.

A teenage girl who looked much like Natalia—but with her father's eyes and hair—crossed her arms and said, half-sternly, "You and Dad have told us that a thousand times, Mom."

"Well, Jenna," Natalia said, giving her daughter a mildly disapproving look, "considering you tried to reveal the location of our getaway two years ago, I have to remind you."

"I said I was sorry," Jenna interrupted quickly. "I just like spending time with both my friends and my family."

"And your father and I understand that," Natalia said gently. "But, Jenna, we also know none of your friends—not even your best one—can keep a secret."

A moment of silence followed until a small boy with dark red hair and red robes spoke up softly.

"Can Mom please finish the story?"

At the boy's words, Natalia paused, trying to remember where she had left off in the story.

Just as she was about to speak, her daughter Jenna said curiously, "Can I ask you something before you go on, Mom?"

"Of course," Natalia replied with a gentle smile.

"Well," Jenna began, "at the beginning of your story, you and Dad grew up in the Human Realm hating each other. Then, when you followed him here, you found out who he really was—and everything changed between you two. Why?"

Her question made all of her brothers and sisters turn toward her in surprise.

Natalia hesitated for a moment, her expression softening with unease.

"Even though your father has long since forgiven me for the things I did, those memories still haunt me to this day. And I hope," she said, pausing for a breath, "that none of you ever repeat the mistakes I made in my past."

Her children quickly promised they wouldn't.

"Good," Natalia said, smiling again. "And as I was saying, yes, your father and I used to hate each other—but, as strange as it sounds, sometimes two people who start off hating each other can end up together."

All of her children looked puzzled, which made her laugh softly.

"It does happen, more often than you'd think—both here in this realm and in the Human Realm as well."

She then continued, "Your father and I spent five wonderful months on our honeymoon. It was the best time of our lives, and we wished it could have lasted forever. But we both had duties and responsibilities to the Magical Realm. And since I was now queen, I needed to learn everything I could to be a great ruler—like your father."

"Did the job ever get to you, Mom?" Mason asked, his tone filled with sympathy.

Natalia smiled at him and said, "Once or twice. But your father always helped me through it—especially since Campbell and his minions were no longer a problem."

"What happened to him?" asked one of the girls, who had dark hair and wore bright green robes.

Turning to her daughter, Natalia replied, "Well, after your father and I took their magic away and banished them to the Human Realm..."

The girl leaned forward eagerly.

"What did they do after that?"

It took Natalia a while to respond, because even mentioning Campbell made her jaw tighten and her blood boil.

Finally, with clear disgust in her voice, she said, "Well, Rosa, a few years after your father and I got married—and after your older brother was born—we learned that Campbell and his minions had become top managers at a local human supermarket. There, they made life miserable for the teenagers who worked under them. At one point, they treated one boy in particular—who later transferred to another store—terribly."

Her children asked what they had done to him. Natalia sighed, her anger simmering beneath the surface.

"All this boy wanted when he came to their store was to start fresh. But he was set up by a cruel, jealous girl—an awful, spiteful human—who couldn't stand that others liked him and not her. No matter how hard the boy tried, Campbell and his followers watched and waited for the right moment to finish what she had started, until they finally forced him to quit his job."

All her children looked horrified.

When Natalia tried to return to her story, Jenna spoke up, curiosity bright in her eyes.

"What happened to the boy after he was forced to quit?"

Natalia smiled gently and said, "He spent every minute of every day searching for a new job in the Human Realm. Unfortunately, those were hard times—since powerful, wealthy humans rarely cared about those who worked hard just to survive. But the real reason he wanted a job was so he could move out of his parents' house and get away from everything that made him hate the Human Realm."

When she reached the end of her story, her son Mason asked, "Did the boy ever get his wish?"

Natalia smiled softly and said, "Well, when your father saw how badly that boy was struggling, it reminded him of what his own life had been like before he ended his second life in the Human Realm. So, he sent a few of our people to bring the boy here while he slept—and gave him a new home in the Magical Realm."

She went on to explain where they had seen him before, and how his life in the Magic Realm was far better than anything he'd ever known in the Human Realm.

When she finished, Natalia looked around at her children and asked if they had any other questions.

Rosa raised her hand.

"What happened to our grandparents?" she asked.

It was a question Natalia had hoped would never come up—but she had promised never to hide the truth from her children.

"Well," she began slowly, "as I've said before, when your father and I were married, our lives in the Human Realm were erased."

All of them looked shocked. Jenna was the first to speak.

"Mom... does that mean neither your parents nor Dad's—"

"Yes, my dear," Natalia interrupted gently, though her voice trembled. "And to be honest, your father and I didn't care. Their lives—especially my parents'—were easier after we were gone. They never went bankrupt or lost everything, and..."

She trailed off, her voice breaking slightly. But her children could already see the sadness in her eyes—and they understood exactly what she meant.

Hoping to cheer her up, Mason said, "Is that why you don't spoil us, Mom? Why you and Dad only give us what we want if we earn it?"

Natalia smiled and nodded.

"Exactly. Every one of you reminds me so much of your father—and of myself. That's why I'm always afraid I might see even a trace of the horrible girl I once was in any of you. When I was pregnant with your brother, I promised myself I would never allow any of my children to make the same terrible mistakes I made when I was young."

"This brings me to say something important. When we're young, we all make mistakes and bad choices—I made plenty myself. But as long as you learn from them, you have no reason to hold yourself back. Sometimes, the best thing you can do is guide someone you care about down a better path than the one you took—gently, and with patience."

Natalia looked around at her children. When she saw that no one had any more questions, she said, "As the years went by and I adjusted to this new life, your father and I started talking about having all of you—which, I suppose, brings this story to an end."

Her children groaned, clearly disappointed that the tale was over.

Before they could complain, Natalia glanced out the window and said, "It's getting late. Off to bed, all of you."

They began to whine in protest, which made her raise her voice just slightly.

"Some of you have school in the morning, and others have lessons or events to attend. And your father and I have a meeting with the land leaders, so—off you go."

Reluctantly, they all got up. The moment they stepped into the hallway, they nearly bumped into Siberanna and a few other attendants.

Smiling, Natalia said, "Could you take my children to their rooms, please?"

"At once, Your Majesty," Siberanna replied with a bow, then nodded to the attendants as a message to attend to the children.

As the children disappeared down another corridor with their escorts, Natalia and Siberanna walked together up a flight of stairs.

"Heading to bed, Your Majesty?" Siberanna asked.

"Oh yes," Natalia began with a yawn, "I'm absolutely exhausted. I just want to crawl into bed with my husband and enjoy what peace we have until tomorrow."

Hearing this made Siberanna feel a bit guilty.

"You know, Your Majesty," she said softly, "I can always reschedule tomorrow's meeting if you and the king—"

"No, Siberanna," Natalia interrupted gently. "This needs to be done. Besides, if we finish it, maybe we'll manage a short rest afterward."

Siberanna sighed.

"My queen, you know none of us like seeing you and the king so overworked."

Natalia smiled wearily.

"It's all part of the job."

They both laughed at that, and neither spoke again until they reached the corridor leading to the royal chambers.

As Natalia turned toward her room, Siberanna said, "Goodnight, Your Majesty."

"Goodnight, Siberanna," Natalia replied warmly before heading down the hall.

When she entered her room a few moments later, she saw that Jason was still awake.

She climbed into bed beside him and he asked, "Did they enjoy the story?"

"They did," she replied with a smile as she laid her head on his chest.

A comfortable silence settled between them before Jason said, "I wish I'd been there to help tell it."

Natalia kissed his cheek.

"You spend more time with them than anyone, love. But they knew this would be a busy week for you. And besides, whoever said ruling a realm was easy?"

They both chuckled quietly, then fell silent again until Natalia murmured, "Once this week is over, things might finally calm down. We can relax and spend more time with the children."

She trailed off, unsure of what else to say, but Jason leaned over and kissed her softly a few times before whispering, "This is why I love you, Natalia. And yes, I know I've said it before, but I'll say it again—you always know the right thing to say."

"And right now," she interrupted with a sleepy smile, "the right thing to say is, let's get some sleep."

They shifted closer, finding a comfortable position.

"I just hope tomorrow's meeting doesn't take all day," she murmured.

"Me neither," Jason said with a chuckle. "But let's not worry about it now. Let's just enjoy a good night's sleep."

And with that, they dimmed the lights and drifted off together—peaceful, content, and without a second thought.

ABOUT THE AUTHOR

ALEXANDER SAUNDERS

Alexander Saunders was born in Portsmouth, England, and later moved with his family to Massachusetts, USA, where he grew up—experiencing life on both sides of the Pond. Diagnosed with autism at a young age, Alexander found that writing became both a passion and a lifeline.

His prolific imagination, nurtured from childhood into adulthood, has helped him cope not only with autism but also with many of life's challenges. Like the characters in his fantasy stories, those difficult times have shaped the person he has become. Writing has given him the opportunity to explore new worlds and endless possibilities through creativity and imagination.

A lifelong admirer of dinosaurs, Alexander also holds a deep fascination with the mysteries of the universe. He believes that life exists beyond our world—and perhaps even on other planets within our own solar system.